Afterall

a novella by
LEE KVERN

© Lee Kvern 2005

All rights reserved. The use of any part of this publication reproduced, transmitted in any form or by any means, electronic, mechanical, recording or otherwise, or stored in a retrieval system, without the prior consent of the publisher is an infringement of the copyright law. In the case of photocopying or other reprographic copying of the material, a licence must be obtained from ACCESS the Canadian Reprography Collective before proceeding.

Library and Archives Canada Cataloguing in Publication
Kvern, Lee, 1957-
Afterall / Lee Kvern.

ISBN 1-897142-01-3
I. Title.

PS8621.V47A64 2005   C813'.6   C2004-907265-X

Cover image: Paul Rasporich, after Degas's "The Tub."

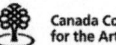

Canada Council   Conseil des Arts
for the Arts   du Canada

Brindle & Glass is pleased to thank the Canada Council for the Arts and the Alberta Foundation for the Arts for their contributions to our publishing program.

Brindle & Glass Publishing
www.brindleandglass.com

1 2 3 4 5   08 07 06 05

PRINTED AND BOUND IN CANADA

For my smalls, my tall, my mother(s).

※ 1 ※

Beth has dinner at Mabel's house tonight. It's the usual gathering of stray friends, mostly misfits and singles, collected from various places: some that Mabel works with, others, like Beth, who Mabel met at the Safeway where Beth delivers milk for Dairyland.

It's the colour of her skin, Beth thinks as she watches her move across the hardwood floor. Beautiful, smooth skin the colour of maple syrup, and not only that, but the pretty, able-bodied line that curves slightly from the bottom of Mabel's breast down to her runner's hips. *Maple*, Beth calls her in her mind. She reminds Beth of the trees in Kitsilano, the lovely trees, and the streets named after the trees in Vancouver: Chestnut, Walnut, Elm, Cypress, and Maple. Maple is half Japanese and half Croatian. She has a husband, Carl. He's from Hamilton. He's the colour of straw.

Maple is a scientist and does research for UBC. Beth isn't sure what kind of research it is – stem cell, biomechanics or something – Beth can never quite remember, but she knows it doesn't involve animals because Maple is a strict vegan. Beth notices nothing made at Dairyland ever finds its way into Maple's shopping cart. One, because Maple knows how enzymes react with other enzymes and which ones are good to combine and which aren't, and two, because Maple loves animals as much as she loves people. Beth is grateful for Maple's loves.

As Beth looks around the dining room table at the group of women assembled there, she decides that Carl and Maple have made the decision that Beth may, in fact, be lesbian and this is the reason Beth is, at thirty-six, unmarried and working as much overtime as she can get her hands on. What Carl and Maple have based this conclusion on Beth has no idea; it's been months since she's dated either sex.

Beth has noticed that over the last few dinners the number of homeless (meaning *merely renting*) men has been on the decrease while the number of own-their-own-condominiums-on-False Creek women has increased. Maple and Carl live in Kerrisdale, but in an older, modest house. The six women around the table are mostly professionals like Maple: a CGA who works for CCRA and has hair like bleached spun sugar, reminding Beth slightly of an albino, with the exception of the mauve eyes on her whitish face. A divorce lawyer – in her late thirties, Beth guesses – who has sworn off unions of any sort completely, partially due to the negotiation of several thousand break-ups over the years, where no one save the lawyer comes out ahead. "And really, what is the point? It all ends badly, anyway." The lawyer looks around the table. No one responds, except for Carl, who shoots a look across the table at Maple. Maple smiles and passes the lawyer a skewer of grilled oyster mushrooms and jalapeño peppers. "Try these," Maple says, "you might like them." A woman with a nose ring sits next to Carl and a couple of other congenial but resigned-looking women in their late forties who have worked in the offices at UBC for twenty years and will probably work another twenty without even noticing.

All the women at the table are remotely pleasant, but not one of them could hold a natural-made beeswax candle to Maple's exotic looks and liberal heart.

Straw-coloured Carl passes the roasted red pepper dip across the table to Beth.

"How's the cow business?" he asks.

"Moo-ing along," Beth says. She doesn't care anymore what people think of her job. She makes OK money: eighteen-ninety-four an hour. Nothing to sneer at but nothing to write home about to her three-time-divorced mother, either. Beth thinks about her mother and *three-time-divorced* like a competitor in the Olympics as if marriage is sport; marriage, which was, at this very moment, supposedly under siege by the gay community. The sanctity of marriage, what a sham. With an attrition rate of fifty percent, and her own Liz Taylor-like mother and the divorce lawyer across the table, Beth can hardly think of marriage as a safe haven in need of preservation by heterosexuals. Yet another good reason not to climb off the fence.

Maple settles down at the table and brings up tonight's topic of discussion. The homeless. And Maple doesn't mean men who only rent. There's no particular agenda for these gatherings, and the clientele (Beth likes to call them, although she's been coming long enough that she now considers herself *friend*) changes on a regular basis. A few regular couples with their young children careering around the living room because Maple has thoughtfully thought to feed them first so that they can ramble about the house terrorizing a) one another and b) Carl's unsociable cat that won't let even their own son, Mason, pet it.

Mason is nine years old in Grade Six. He skipped a grade based on his premature grasp of everything that came home in his Grade Four scribblers. Like he'd done it a million times already and frankly the review was overkill. But he's a funny kid. Oddly quiet and extremely shy, wears a hoodie over his face most of the time, intensely intellectual and hugely aware of a large number of social issues for a nine-year-old kid. Although Beth supposes Mason comes by his knowledge honestly; both his parents are recycled-card-carrying environmentalists. Beth remembers when Carl had himself chained to a hundred-year-old tree last year up at Clayoquot Sound. *Had himself chained* to a tree by someone else, Carl explained, as opposed to chaining himself to a tree. Like he was the hostage, the casualty, the captive, much like the tree that was about to be mown down by MacMillan Bloedel and not the other way around – not simply another aggressive environmentalist.

"It has a psychological effect on the guys on the Cats. They aren't really sure if you're one of the protesters or just some poor stiff who's been forced into sacrificing his own skin for the bark of a hundred-year-old tree," Carl smiles. "They back off every time." His picture was plastered all over the front of the *Vancouver Sun*, Carl chained to a tree and looking suitably worried, strictly for the drama, with a big Cat not three feet away.

Mason goes to a school that specializes in mathematics. For snack he takes Rubbermaid containers of roasted soybean and fresh-shelled garden peas while all the other kids feast on Fruit Roll-ups and Fruit Gushers, not an ounce of nutrition in them and look at how those sugar enzymes and Number 40 red dye go straight to the part of the brain that throws them into hyper-mode. According to science and straight from the lovely lips of Maple, sugar is Satan's brother-in-law.

Mason is restrained and comes up to whisper in

Maple's ear. He's at the age where his two front teeth look like a rabbit's in comparison to the surrounding baby teeth. He bites his top lip constantly as if trying to cover them.

"Mason would like me to tell you about the man that lives behind his school. The man lives in a Styrofoam box that the janitor left outside from the new water heater they put in the school last year," Maple says and hugs Mason to her side. Why no one has removed the box after an entire year escapes Beth, but she figures it might have something to do with empathy. The kind of school spirit that supports the disadvantaged.

"Mason and I pack an extra lunch every day for him to take for the man," Maple says. Beth can only imagine what the lunch is: organic lentil soup with sun-baked rye bread and a couple of freshly peeled parsnips. Exactly what every homeless person requires after too many bottles of Baby Duck and Wild Turkey bourbon, and the odd Wendy's Big Bacon Classic salvaged from the garbage. A veritable healthful feast in a brown paper bag delivered by a boy who cannot speak without his mother. Beth wonders how Mason manages in school. Mason blushes beneath his hood and stands there quietly enjoying the warmth of his mother. Everyone enjoys the warmth of your mother, Beth wants to tell him, surveying the table. And your mother's kindness.

If it weren't for Maple, Beth would be sitting at home watching another night of Discovery Channel or Bravo! or WTN, or heading down to Benny's on Broadway to meet the same two single women she's been meeting there for the last five years, Laurel and Gwen from Dairyland. Beth has never been very comfortable with children, not because she doesn't like them but because she hasn't been around many. She's not quite sure what to do with them. They're so spontaneous, unpredictable. She's afraid they might combust and she won't know how to put them out. Regardless, Beth smiles at Mason. He doesn't smile back. Maple does because she knows Mason means to; she's his official interpreter.

The dinner ranges from homemade hummus and Indian flatbread to strips of marinated steak that Carl has generously grilled for the non-vegans. The discussion circles around the homeless. The woman with the ring through her nose, who runs Buddha's Belly, a strictly organic vegetarian restaurant on West Fourth, thinks that being on the street is largely a choice you make. No such thing as bad luck or down-on-your-karma, or that life on the street might be better than life at home, or mental illness even. Just the sheer stupidity of your own bad choices. Nose Ring, who has eaten most of the hummus and flatbread, and is sitting at the end of the table next to Carl, is in conflict with Carl's bleeding-heart (her words) views. She has short-cropped orange hair and Beth is sure Dairyland would never hire her with that ringed piece of metal through her nose. Beth has a third glass of Cabernet, pushes the last piece of steak around on her plate, and tries to ignore Nose Ring and her Clairol Number 14.5 dye. Her hair looks like Halloween.

"I had a guy harass me for money once on Granville Street," Nose Ring says. "He was so incensed that I wouldn't shell out my hard-earned money to him, I thought he might punch me right there on the corner. I looked down at his shoes, his two-hundred-and-fifty-dollar Fluevogs. Fluevogs is a high-end shoe store on Granville," Nose Ring adds for the two office women, who, from the look of their leather Reeboks, have never stepped foot outside The Bay.

"Anyways, I said, '*sell your shoes, man.*' Let me tell you, that shut him up pretty quick. I have no sympathy for the homeless; they're all drug addicts and crackheads looking for an easy way out. Why don't they get a job like everyone else and buy their own damn wine?"

Nose Ring raises her glass of wine as if in a toast to the crackheads and drug addicts who are living the free and easy life on the streets of Vancouver, but she's so obnoxious that even the disillusioned lawyer next to Beth, who might have agreed, doesn't join in. Nose Ring drinks alone.

Carl looks sideways at Nose Ring and doesn't venture anything in retort. From the expression on Maple's face, she may not invite this one back again. No one says anything. Maple steers the conversation neatly off to the pros and cons of spiking trees. Eager to avoid further transgression from Nose Ring, the table jumps in.

But too late for Beth. Nose Ring has found Beth's goat and has wrapped her stubby fingers around its neck. Beth finishes her glass of wine and pours another one. This is the Year of the Goat, Beth thinks. If there is one thing Beth is sure of, regardless of whether she will marry male or reside with a life partner, a Large Marge, a Big Judy complete with leather and lace, is her compassion for humankind in general. Clearly, Nose Ring has the empathy of canned smelts. Beth rises unsteadily to her feet and lifts her glass of Cabernet into the air.

"In commiseration of goats and the homeless, I am going to spend a night on the street," Beth waves her wine glass around. Recently she read about a journalist who spent an entire year in a big city shantytown in order to write a book on the homeless. Mind you, Beth recalls, he'd had a series of life's misdemeanors that eventually lead him to believe that living in Tent City in Toronto would be preferable to your own home.

The table stops in mid-sentence, tree spiking and Husqvarna chainsaws aside, everyone stares in amazement. Nose Ring is glaring holes on the wall behind Beth's swaying body.

"Well," says Carl, looking at her as if she's either commendable or committable. Mason hovers around his mother again, whispering secrets in her ear to share with the world.

"I want to come, too," Maple says, then stammers and looks at Mason. His cheeks are flushed. Beth's heart does a tiny jig – *Maple* wants to go?

"I mean, *he* wants to go," Maple says, and even Carl looks shocked.

Beth stares at Maple and thinks she sees a momentary gleam of apprehension, or is it admiration? And even though children have never before been on Beth's radar screen, lately at Safeway Beth has found herself noticing the rash of fresh spring babies being pushed along in shopping carts by exhausted but elated mothers.

It's admiration, Beth decides, looking at Maple. The path to a man's heart is through his stomach, Beth thinks, watching Carl help himself to another skewer of Maple's grilled oyster mushrooms. Then certainly the trail to a woman's lies in the heart of her children. Mason. Beth can do this. She can do this for Maple. Lovely, beautiful-skinned Japanese-Croatian Maple. She rallies herself to the idea. "Of course, we won't go homeless down in Oppenheimer Park or Victory Square off Cambie, or anywhere remotely dangerous," Beth says. Victory Square, what a kick in the ass. Come to Vancouver, fall into the depths of humanity, get hooked on heroin and have nothing to look forward to other than getting fitted for dentures at age thirty-something when your teeth finally fall out. That is, if you can afford them. That and sleeping beneath benches in the park.

Carl rises to refill everyone's wine glass and Maple busies herself passing out individual bowls of crème brûlée made miraculously with soy milk. No, they will not go anywhere hazardous, Beth thinks. After all a thirty-six-year-old woman who works at Dairyland and hasn't dated anything in the last four months, and a nine-year-old boy who wears a hoodie over his face and whispers in his mother's ear, may not, in actuality, have their street legs firmly beneath them.

Nose Ring remarks to Carl that Beth couldn't last an hour on the street, let alone a whole night, but Carl is with Beth on this one. He ignores the woman.

"I think I know where Mason's sleeping bag is," Carl says, "and it's a good one, too, a MEC we got on special. I can dig it out for this long weekend, if you like." He looks at Beth.

Beth glances over at Maple. Maple looks tired suddenly, as if the years of protest have extracted their price from her lovely face. But surely this is their intent is, isn't it? Aren't Maple and Carl attempting to raise the bar on life issues? Issues that go straight to the heart of humanity? Straight to the heart of Mason's global education? Really, what could be more fitting than letting a nine-year-old boy spend a night on the streets in the Homeless Capital of Canada?

Maple runs her smooth hands up and down Mason's thin back like she is embedding the fortitude of motherhood within him to take out onto the precarious streets of Vancouver. On the same streets, Maple has protested pro-lifers and summit meetings, Expos and premiers who own fantasylands, seal hunts and Wal-Marts, logging companies and Starbucks. Maple is rubbing Mason's back now with all the fervour of a massage therapist. The boy relaxes into her.

"Well, isn't this terrific," Maple says. Though to Beth's eye, she's not entirely convinced how terrific it is. Carl, she notices, seems to be hovering, waiting, perhaps for a cue from her. Maple smiles reassuringly and continues to stroke Mason's spine with both hands. Carl smiles at Nose Ring, but Nose Ring ignores him and pushes her coarse, orange-dyed hair behind one ear, revealing a curved line of ordinary safety pins. Not earrings or studs or real silver but everyday out-of-the-bathroom-vanity safety pins. They look like they hurt. She's got eleven in all.

Beth, at the other end of the table, is not sure either, but it's flown out of her mouth and she'll be damned if Nose Ring will see her with anything other than soy crème brûlée on her face.

The guy that is truly homeless parks himself daily in front of the Chinese grocer's on the corner of Broadway and Larch. Benny's is next door, a funky little place that sells bagels and beer and stays open late into the night. It's a hotspot for the young and activist-oriented crowd, Maple's crowd, which is why it is also a hotspot for the guy next door in front of the Chinese grocer's. People who pay attention to social issues tend to buy newspapers. Not to mention have empathy for the homeless — and regardless of whether they actually read the newspaper or not, it's a guilt-free way for them to give a hand-out. Beth has seen him for years, at least the last few that she can recall, wandering up and down from Kitsilano Beach back up to as far as Kerrisdale in the early morning and then, later in the evening, on to Broadway, blue-bin diving, sifting through the sanitation barrels bolted down on the sidewalk every forty feet or so, looking for pop bottles or leftover take-outs from the Benny's or the Chinese.

And this May long weekend, Queen Victoria's birthday, is no exception. While Beth finishes up her last delivery for Dairyland at the Chinese grocers, and also runs errands in preparation for her and Mason's homeless night on the street, he's here on the corner.

He spends a full eight hours out front of the corner store selling copies of *Word on the Street,* a newspaper produced by the homeless, written by the homeless and sold by the homeless, but printed by the big *Vancouver Sun* conglomerates, the proceeds of which go back into the writing, producing and selling of this newspaper. Hence a job for the homeless. A reason, Beth thinks, to drag yourself off the back stairs of the all-night laundromat, or if you're lucky, the men's shelter off Main, and plop yourself down on the front side of the street where the people who live in decent but exorbitantly priced flats or old Kitsilano houses converted into eight apartment suites, live and breathe and thrive. In short where the homeful people are. And some of them buy newspapers. Beth is one of them.

Not because she's overly interested in reading what the word on the street is, or even if there is word on the street. The *Word on the Street* sounds sinister – reminds her of things like drug deals or the next big heist when the Chinese grocer's will get hijacked for their four hundred and forty-some dollars in the till after a brisk morning of selling Dentyne Ice and bottles of Cherry Coke and white cranberry juice, bags of Doritos and the odd pack of cigarettes. Cigarettes for those mad enough to still smoke in the face of all the gruesome cigarette package warnings and strong moral ads on television that make anyone smoking akin to a modern-day leper. Every now and then, Beth foregoes the pictorial still-life documentary of blackened lungs and bleeding gums and premature babies and indulges in a slim-papered stick of leprosy herself. But only when she's out indulging in other social faux-pas, such as drinking more Sleeman's than the legal limit allows and then covertly making her way along the back alleys in her small red Fiat to her suite in the basement of her newly-renovated house behind Benny's. She rents the main floor out to a young married couple, who make love three times a week and twice on the weekends above her strictly-for-sleeping bed. Their rent almost covers the full mortgage.

Beth buys the newspaper every week, and if she happens to do deliveries twice in one week to the Chinese grocer, then she buys it twice. Today she notices that the man has on a zip-up coat that she hasn't seen him wear before, and the coat has a name embroidered on it: *Kenneth*. His name is Kenneth. Kenneth has long corn-coloured hair and a beard that would serve any Shakespearean actor well, except his is gnarled and grungy, stained by too many years of living beneath park benches and in tunnels and abandoned doorways, on the bare black asphalt. Beth hands him a toonie in exchange for *The Word* even though it only costs a loonie.

And today, beyond Kenneth's usual, shy nod of his woolly-bearded head, and brief glance into her eyes, Beth looks into his eyes, really looks this time. Perhaps it's because he has a name, something concrete she can attach her sympathy to. *Oh, do you know Kenneth, who sells newspapers for a living on Broadway?* she can hear herself asking the clientele at Maple's next dinner. As if she knows the man now, the man she has bought newspapers from every week for the past four years, perhaps even has some personal slant on behalf of one homeless person, if not a partial spokesperson for the majority. She has no idea how Kenneth might have ended up on this corner and where he resides when he's not here.

It makes her think of her five-month stint on the Inner-city Search and Rescue team. After all the fundamental exercises and first aid courses and mock searches and water rescue preparation and avalanche training (*avalanches in the inner city?*) the only real search Beth went on was for a seven-year-old girl. She remembers scouring the streets around English Bay, with her heart in her mouth, ready at any moment to find the likely, small-framed girl in a lifeless heap beneath a pile of garbage in a dingy back alley. When, in fact, halfway through the search, the girl turned out to be fifteen but was developmentally delayed and had the capacity of a seven-year-old. Misinformation on the part of the Vancouver Police. Quite by accident, when Beth stopped into one of the dozen Starbucks along Robson Street to order an iced Americano, she overheard the fifteen-year-old girl trying to hire a cab to take her to Disneyland. Beth retired shortly after, though she still keeps her ready pack in the trunk of her Fiat should she, herself, happen to get marooned on Robson. Or the time Beth volunteered for Homecare and drove once a week out to Port Coquitlam to help bathe an elderly man who had lived in the same house for eighty-seven years. The man, whose penis resembled a dried up seahorse and posed no threat of danger and/or embarrassment to either Beth or the man, a simple fact of age, protested his bath each time. Out of her fourteen weeks' service, Beth only managed to bathe the man three times. After a while, she couldn't bear the stench and didn't go back.

All those years and she never truly looked at this man. Kenneth. She sees Kenneth's blue irises skating about in his head, the colour of his eyes so vibrant and intense in comparison to his weathered aged face (even though he's probably close to her own age) that it startles her momentarily. She is the first to look away. Odd, she thinks that she never noticed that before. Has never seen him as anything more than an object of misfortune. It's a pity that people can be reduced to the status of an object, like that great lamp that Beth just had to have from Urban Barn that she put on her shelf in the living room. Now familiar and in its proper place, all it does is collect dust and ceases to be of interest to anyone.

"Thanks, Ken," she says, handing him a toonie. Feeling entitled, she supposes, to shorten his name to the familiar because she has bought so many *Words* over the past few years that she could probably write *Word on the Street* herself, although she barely skims the articles, mostly peruses the amateur photographs of events that have already happened in the West End that she's missed out on because she's working overtime whenever she can get it.

Kenneth says, "My name is not Ken."

Beth points to his coat as evidence, as if perhaps Kenneth has lost his street sense or had a particularly sleepless night on the street.

"No," Kenneth says. "I found it at the Sarmy. It's not my coat."

"The Sarmy?" Beth looks puzzled.

He points down the block at the Salvation Army. Beth nods, it's a nice coat; too bad it isn't his name. Though she supposes that furthers her theory of everything in its proper place, a Mary Poppins approach to the world. That objects, like people, need to be named and categorized and sorted into their suitable places, like Oppenheimer Park or Victory Square, so that they can go unnoticed and quietly collect dust. Less trouble that way. She knows the only reason Kenneth is allowed his invisibility on Broadway is because he's selling *Word on the Street* and not randomly accosting people for their money. She waits for Kenneth to tell her his real name but Kenneth does not offer it up. He seems to have forgotten that they were talking at all and goes back to surveying the sidewalk for dropped change or a decent-sized cigarette butt he can smoke later on.

"See you later, Kenneth," Beth says. Kenneth looks up, surprised, like she's a potential new customer and raises his copies of *Word on the Street* to her.

"Next week," Beth says.

At 4:00 PM sharp, after a full day of deliveries for Dairyland and turning down an overtime shift, Beth drives over to Carl and Maple's. It's as good a night as

any to go homeless. Besides, she wants to go before the steam runs out of her current, spur-of-the-moment passion. Clear skies, the Queen's birthday, and Mason will have Sunday and Monday off to recoup before school. She and Mason pack a few things in Safeway plastic bags for authenticity and to remain anonymous. It wouldn't do to go ambling down Broadway with a Martha Stewart yellow, lime-green, and blue plaid overnight bag. They have their MEC sleeping bags that Carl fished out of the basement after dinner last night. Mason asks Maple to ask Beth if he can bring a flashlight but Beth thinks it may attract unwanted attention so Mason takes it back into his clutter of a bedroom. Beth peeks in and sees hundreds of labelled jars and shelves. He must have his mother's sense of curiosity, her love of exploring what's beneath the surface, as well as his Einstein mathematic smarts. Carl drags out a couple of those aluminum fold-out-flat canvas lawn chairs. If Mason can manage to carry the sleeping bags and one Safeway bag, then Beth can easily tuck the lightweight chairs under her arm.

Like all good campers, Beth and Mason decide to choose their site before going off in search of sustenance.

Broadway is too busy, too open, too many people move up and down the sidewalks all night; she knows this because when she's been working too much overtime and occasion strikes her once or even three times a week, then she wanders up Broadway herself and has too many beer at Benny's. Beth finds various nooks and suitable doorways and back alley crannies, but their closeness makes her think they would be better off somewhere open, somewhere predictable. Somewhere safe. She's got a dependent to think of. A dependent that won't speak to her but simply gazes up earnestly displaying his two big bunny teeth. It makes Beth want to laugh but then she'd have to explain to Mason that it's because he looks so sweet and marvellously awkward before the onset of puberty moves in and changes him into a sombre-looking young man who will have to whisper in his mother's ear when he wants to take a girl to a movie. No, Beth thinks, Mason would not find this remotely funny or cute. He's a serious lot.

The two of them wander up and down the tree-named streets of Kitsilano, up Cypress, down Walnut, Chestnut, and even along Maple. Beth can't find what she's looking for. But then on the quiet suburban corner of something and MacDonald, Mason finds a construction zone. The intersection is blocked off on all four sides for sewer repair or whatever those overpaid city workers do beneath the paved roads of Vancouver. You can't go deeper than sea level — the ocean's just a few blocks down the street, so they can't be working *that* hard for their twenty-two bucks an hour, Beth thinks. She's applied with the city numerous times and can't get on. She's still annoyed about it. It's 4:30 and like clockwork the city workers are packing up and vacating the work site. Beth and Mason stand down the block beneath the large overgrown chestnut trees that form a live swaying green roof for as far as Beth can see down the street.

It's perfect, she thinks as they make their way to the corner. A fort surrounded on all four sides by an overkill of signs: Sewer Repair, No Exit, Detour, Danger! Mason steps inside and circles the square fort. Beth sets down the aluminum chairs but doesn't unfold them. It is perfect. The manhole cover has been replaced, there's no obnoxious odour, rather the gentle salt air of the ocean mixes with the nutty scent of the chestnut trees. She looks at the four corner houses and seems to remember that a prominent writer lives around here. A writer with a social conscience. She's seen him interviewed on TV. He travels to places like India and Argentina and volunteers for Amnesty International, she thinks. Surely he would be sympathetic with their homage to the homeless? Writers do that sort of thing all the time, don't they – metaphorically try on other people's shoes?

Beth looks up and down the street while Mason walks the inside perimeter of the fort. Why, Beth wonders, is it all right to be homeless in downtown Vancouver, but not, say, in Point Grey, an upscale neighbourhood just down the street? Although she knows the answer to that question. Proper placement is the key. Know your agreed-upon territory. Beth knows this is probably not agreed upon by anyone but her and Mason. She decides it is too early and too light to set up camp just yet.

"Want to go get something to eat?" Beth asks.

Mason nods shyly.

Beth hides their shopping bag full of tonight's pyjamas and tomorrow's change of clothes and toothbrushes and six-pack of Evian and a couple of veggie bars, hoping that no one will come upon their stash while they are out foraging for food. She understands the practicality (and, no doubt, status) of having your own shopping cart, but looking up and down the suburban street, there's not one in sight. There's a Perego double stroller out in front of one of the houses, but they didn't come out here to be thieves, they came out to be homeless. Beth doesn't feel like lugging their stuff around anymore. She'll leave it there and take her chances.

An older man with a neatly trimmed moustache walks by with a Pekinese on an expandable lease. The small dog is enormously interested in Mason and his new fort and wants to leap the signs to find a way in. Thankfully the man is embarrassed by his dog's persistence and pulls the dog swiftly along by its neck, not bothering himself to be curious about why Beth and Mason might be there. Beth wonders if she should post another sign that reads, 'We are here for the night in sympathy with the homeless. No one need be bothered by us, we will be gone by morning.' No, too wordy. Perhaps just a No Danger! sign would work. But that would negate the whole reason they are out here. It makes it more valid when you must duck and cover, not only from the police, but those nasty homeowners, and drunks roving the streets after the bars close looking for someone to beat up for the heck of it. The homeless are perfect targets, Beth thinks. Perfectly harmless, too. But like everything else, Beth knows there are always the few bad ones who make the whole world live like everyday is a re-enactment of the six o'clock evening news. All home invasions and car accidents, house siding scams and rapes and drive-by shootings and murders of helpless people. She must be careful for herself, but above all for Mason. Mason watches the dog that keeps trying to double back to him and his fort, and smiles for the first time since they left Maple and Carl's in Kerrisdale.

Beth glances over at the windows of the corner houses. The curtains are shut against the late-afternoon sun, and hopefully no one will spot their campsite before dark and call the police. One of them, she is sure now, is that writer, although his name escapes her. Friesen? Freehart? Frasier? No, that's a TV show, never mind. The idea of the writer comforts her, makes her feel more secure. He is a man with an eye out for the world and he may watch their goings-on. They could find themselves the subject of a short story someday: *Popular Homeless* or *Telling My Homeless Lies* or *As For Me and My Homeless*.

She realizes what a precarious existence it is for the homeless. While she owns an older house behind Benny's, and has renters to boot, technically making her a land baron, a nasty homeowner, she also has curtains on every window that are pleasant and white, raw cotton, entirely utilitarian, but curtains nonetheless that she can close when it's dark and sleep in relative safety. And even though people camp nightly next door in the temporarily vacant lot beside her house, the only thing she ever calls, never the police, is a cab on her way to work so as not to jeopardize her parking spot out front.

Beth and silent Mason walk up Broadway to the White Spot. They are homeless, but homeless with American Express and a food allowance. Beth knows for certain that Mason has never been inside White Spot, too much grease and cow and lactose, and they have those do-it-yourself sundaes complete with sugar-galore artificial strawberry and chocolate fudge toppings. And as much as she loves and appreciates Maple, she takes Mason inside.

And White Spot serves that old black devil, Coca-a-cola. What's that saying? No caffeine until fourteen? Beth remembers Carl reciting it every time one of the clientele mistakenly brought a six-pack of Pepsi or Coke over, and Mason whispered into Maple's ear that he'd like one. Carl didn't even have to hear what Mason was saying, he knew. No caffeine until fourteen. Beth wonders if that applies to meat and sex and beer. If so, Mason's in for a helluva fourteenth birthday. He could get a preview tonight where meat and Coca-a-cola are concerned; a kid needs to live a little before he goes homeless for the night. She looks down at him. He looks worried. Perhaps he knows the crime they are about to commit.

Beth looks over the menu. Mason's eyes flit around the restaurant like he's underage and the cockfight is about to begin. But then he spots the do-it-yourself-sundae bar in the middle of the restaurant and looks a little less anxious but still, he doesn't want to be a full accomplice in the ordering of immoral dishes.

"Would you like the White Spot Special Platter?" Beth asks. "It comes in a pirate ship."

Mason settles his large dark eyes on her. Beth thinks she notes a hint of excited compliance, if not a small degree of piracy, in them. His chance, perhaps, to sample forbidden treasure.

"We'll have two White Spot Specials," Beth tells the waitress, who resembles a twelve-year-old Madonna with full pink lips and a huge gap between her teeth, neither of which she can do anything about but smile. And she does, a lot.

"Well done, and two Cokes, please," Beth says, and then it occurs to her that it's Saturday night and reason enough for occasion. "No, on second thought, make that one Coke and I'll have a glass of red wine." She looks at Mason beneath his hoodie.

Mason will go home tomorrow no longer a virgin vegan, if this is the first time he's had a burger. But for Maple's sake, Beth will not run the risk of E.coli, or worse, mad cow disease.

"Can you get mad cow from an undercooked burger?" Beth asks the waitress.

"No." The girl smiles and shakes her head. "You can only get that in England or Alberta," she says, as if it's a special kind of burger you might want to order.

Beth isn't sure. How would a twelve-year-old Madonna look-alike know?

"At any rate, cook it well," Beth tells her.

Beth looks at Mason to see if any of this has registered. Mason looks unconcerned. Apparently vegans know as much about carnivores as Beth knows about vegans, which is practically nothing. Whenever Beth is asked to bring potluck to Maple's, she stops by Benny's and buys a dozen multigrain bagels. They're kosher. Close enough, she thinks. The young waitress smiles her gapped teeth once more, and leaves.

Beth is surprised when Mason takes his hoodie off. His body is thinner than she thought. Beth knows that Maple doesn't starve him but he's extremely slender for a boy of nine. Mason glances around the room like he's sizing up the North American Fast Food Market. Oh, no, Beth wants to tell him, this is nothing, you should see Burger King and Wendy's and McDonald's! But the kingpin of them all is KFC, good ole Kentucky Colonel Saunders. Dirty bird and fries ready in three minutes flat, dripping with vein-cloggers and glutinous with the reek of grease. You can almost feel it settle on your skin when you walk in, it's that bad. Beth wonders if cholesterol can be transmitted through osmosis.

"We'll have gravy with the fries," she decides,

glancing over at Mason's bird-like body as their waitress goes by with a huge oval tray of burgers and a fold-out stand.

After burgers and fries with gravy, two cokes and two hand-built sundaes, Mason's eyelids start to droop like they might close down and not open again until tomorrow morning. Beth looks out the window at the dusk, deepening, settling in for the night. It must be close to 9:00. She glances at the rooster clock on the wall. 8:47. Three and a half hours? Good god, she's had dates that were shorter than this.

"Well, shall we head home now?"

Mason looks up, startled.

"Right, homeless, I mean."

Mason pulls his hoodie back on and covers his face, readying himself for the night ahead. Beth gets ready by gulping down her fourth glass of wine. On the way down Broadway, Beth glances in the window at Benny's, but it's early yet and the place is half empty. There are a few don't-want-to-go-home-to-their-darling-spouse patrons, which causes Beth to suspect that marriage may be similar to croissants, all fancy and French-sounding but one or two bites in and you know it's just a lot of puffed-up pastry with hot air and excess butter. Beth likes to wait for the out-on-a-Saturday-night-binge crowd. They tend to get smashed but not as badly as the Friday-nighters who know they have all weekend to recuperate. In fact, today happens to be Saturday of the May long weekend when everyone under the age of thirty heads east to Penticton to soak up the sun on Skaha Beach. Beth gave that up when she gave up two-piece swimsuits, after she overheard a strikingly attractive clerk in a funky clothing store comment that beyond age thirty no one wanted to see your sagging breasts, let alone soggy belly. Save that for the young, the girl said. Even though Beth could wear one admirably now if she liked.

They pass the Chinese grocer's on the corner. Kenneth is not there, either. Maybe, he's gone east to Skaha, too? Beth smiles at her own joke and looks down at Mason, who walks alongside her taking large, exaggerated steps like a junkie coming off a high.

"Would you like a piggyback?" Beth asks.

Mason nods from beneath his hoodie. Beth wishes she could cajole a verbal response from him but without his mother there to act as interpreter, well, there's probably not much chance of that. She knows she's in for a long, silent night.

Beth crouches down on the sidewalk and Mason wraps his frail body against her back. Beth stands up. She is not surprised that he is as light as the aluminum chairs. Perhaps she should talk to Maple. Try to get him on a weekly dose of whipping cream. After all, she's been going to Maple's dinners for three years. After all, this is Maple's son she's been entrusted with and is carrying on her back. The boy needs to be a boy, Beth will tell her. Just an ordinary boy. But she knows the minute she looks into Maple's soft, intelligent eyes, her concern will dissolve and she will be placated. For a moment she feels awful about taking Mason to the White Spot and hopes that Mason will also feel bad and not whisper it into his mother's ear when they get home.

On the corner of MacDonald and something, Beth can't read the street sign anymore, the sun has set on Kitsilano beach, and the latticed trees mask the streetlights overhead. Beth finds the four-way construction site and slides Mason down onto the ground. Mason is barely awake and teeters from side to side until Beth puts her hands on both his shoulders and steadies him.

He opens his eyes and seeing their No Exit, Detour, Sewer Repair, Danger! fort, smiles. Beth smiles at his bunny teeth.

She digs around beneath the signs where she left their Safeway bag and MEC sleeping bags. She can't find them. Perhaps she put them on the opposite side? She fumbles in the dark, not able to see clearly due to the colossal chestnut trees, which while she loved them a minute ago, are getting on her nerves now. She can't find anything but one of the aluminum chairs that she trips over as she scours the fort. The chair seems to have been unfolded wrong and the frame is twisted. Their sleeping bags are gone. So are their pyjamas and clean shorts and underwear and t-shirts for tomorrow, their six-pack of Evian and washcloth and one towel and toothbrushes and Buzz Lightyear toothpaste. Beth looks over at Mason sitting on the asphalt. She can't see his eyes in the dark, but she knows he is shaken. He's got his knees drawn up around his chin and is hugging them. She is shaken, too.

Beth goes over and sits stiffly down beside him. The pavement is still warm from the day. Mason doesn't move.

"Well, I guess this is lesson number one," Beth says, "always find a shopping cart." Beth tries to jostle him with her elbow. Mason doesn't say a word. "Do you want to go home?" she asks. He shakes his head. The word on the street is he wants to be homeless. Beth finds herself filling in imaginary words for him. It's more interesting than the one-way dialogue they've had up until now. She feels like she's out on one of the blind dates her well-meaning friends have set up in the past where she does all the talking and the guy/gal stares at her uselessly. She looks down at Mason and part of her looks down at herself, too. Mason looks exhausted and thin and pale like it's tough being a kid of nine, so intelligent, so highly evolved that the rest of the human race hasn't caught up to him yet. Beth thinks she looks reasonably fit and pleasant enough, but alone, chronically alone like someone has posted a sign on her. Detour. Danger! She wishes she could hold Mason in her arms and comfort herself.

"Well, all right then, take my coat and we'll make you a bed and you can lie down."

Beth struggles to straighten the bent frame of the aluminum chair and manages to get a facsimile of a bowed hammock for Mason to sleep on.

"It'll be warm enough that we can sleep without sleeping bags and besides, if things get rough, I'll go out and rustle us up a *Vancouver Sun* to cover up with," Beth smiles half-heartedly.

Mason says nothing.

Mason lies down and Beth tucks her lightweight fleece around his small body. Soon her thirty-six-year-old buttocks are aching from the asphalt, as warm as it still is. Mason's breathing evens out into sleep. Beth unfolds her legs and stretches into the black air. The air smells like KFC and ocean, grease and salt. What a brief, fast-food life we lead, Beth thinks. She lies back on the asphalt and looks up through the chestnut trees at the few stars that glimmer in-between the dark network of branches. The avenue is quiet; all the house lights are out. She thinks about the sprawling, immaculate homes down the street in Point Grey and equally, the houses in North Van, that are simply out of reach for the average person. The city, itself, is stunning: the flowering cherry trees, the oceans of carrot-coloured tulips down along the boulevards on Robson and English Bay each spring, and Stanley Park with its massive Redwoods and Wreck

Beach with young naked guys in dreadlocks coming by to sell you warm tins of vanilla Coke and hashish, too, while standing over you with their slightly swaying penises. And Deep Cove with honey-dipped doughnuts the size of small tires that they sell in a shop down by the water. She's seen more BMWs and Mercedes Benzes and Hummers than in any other city she's visited. Really, more beauty and wealth combined than one place deserves. They call it Lotus Land, and it's true. It's lush and green, affluent in every sense. She's lucky to live here, even luckier to have a house, however modest. Her thoughts drift back to the asphalt she's lying on and how she'd like something to prop her head up and possibly a warm donut, but Mason has her fleece and the only thing she has are the clothes on her body and her Fluevogs. She takes her shoes off and puts them behind her head. She thinks about the inert breathing bodies of the homeless people on Hastings Street she steps over early mornings when she's delivering milk. She wonders where Kenneth lays his head down at night.

Her eyes adjust to the dark now and she can see Mason's slim chest rise and fall with each breath he takes. They're fine here, she thinks. Just fine. Two homeless people without pyjamas, no change of clothes, no Buzz Lightyear toothpaste, no six-pack — they are fine. It will be an experience they will never forget. Beth's head feels woolly but pleasant from the wine and her eyes threaten to shut but she knows she can't. The responsibility for Carl and Maple's nine-year-old boy is on her shoulders. She can't sleep. She has to lie here and *stand on guard for he*, she sings to the tune of the national anthem. Even though years of living on her own and in big-city Vancouver have taught her that once you've had a key scraped down the length of your new red Fiat, or your house broken into for the DVD player and Compaq computer, then you're usually good for a few months before the next thing.

Beth sits up. She can hear faint voices and music, probably from Jericho Beach, she thinks. She doesn't go there anymore, but she used to. A decade and some ago, though it seems like a lifetime, twenty years old and out on the beach in the dark, beer and guitars and out-of-control bonfires, groups of other twenty-year-olds roaming the sand, just like her, looking for that proper fit, that one person who would embrace you back and turn your life into a life worth refusing overtime work at Dairyland for. It occurs to Beth that those years from twenty to thirty are the charmed ones, the really good years in which to find your comrade. Perhaps the only years.

Beth lies back down on her Fluevogs and stares up at the dark trees. She listens to the distant voices and feels her body drift, falling into the thick sea air, beneath the asphalt, beyond the tangled roots of the chestnut trees, falling, as sleep overtakes her, down to where the city workers aren't repairing sewers but playing crib. She is incensed. Twenty-two bucks an hour to play crib? And they won't hire Beth, who works like a dog? Then she hears the snap of a twig and comes back to the surface of the earth, warm but hard and unforgiving. She sits up and looks around. She looks over at Mason, who has turned on his side now and is breathing with complete and utter abandon as only children can. His small mouth is open, eyes not quite shut and he is breathing for all the world like it is his still-safe oyster. Beth scans the four corners. The street is tranquil and if she listens hard she can hear the waves lap down on Jericho and someone playing Paul McCartney on the guitar. *Let it be, let it be, let it be, let it be*, she hums along and lies back down. She can't remember anything but the chorus of the song. *Speaking words of something*, she thinks but what, she can't recall. The tepid sea air, wine like a good muscle-relaxant, the tender rhythm of Mason's shallow, even breathing mixes in with the far-off lapping drift of the tide. She can't catch herself. It's been so long since anyone breathed beside her for an entire night.

She awakens to cool damp air, a headache and silence. Beth sits up and gets her bearings. Right, homeless. She doesn't know if she's had the maximum efficiency of a seventeen-minute nap or slept for four hours. She wishes she had worn her watch. She wishes she had a tent. Her head is no longer harbouring a pleasing fog, but throbbing dully with the beginning of a mild hangover. She should have drank more or not at all. She listens in the dark for the tide, the voices, the lovely thrumming guitar, but hears nothing. Not a sound. Not even the sound of Mason's breathing.

She stands up quickly, so that she has to stop a

moment and wait for the bits of fluttering lights like fruit flies to clear from her head before she can see down the street. She scans all four corners. She can't see him anywhere. She gets down on her hands and knees and scours the fort once more, in case he's moved over and she's missed him.

She breaks out of the fort, knocking over the Detour sign. She runs full-speed in all directions at once, cutting across the neatly trimmed lawns, scanning the massive rhododendrons and walls of climbing ivy and clematis looking for Mason's small, thin frame. Maybe he had to go to the bathroom? She can't think of any other reason why he'd leave their fort. Surely someone couldn't have waltzed in and simply removed Mason without a struggle, without her hearing. She runs without breathing.

"Mason!" She hisses out into the dark, not wanting to arouse the neighbourhood. Why she cares about that, she's not sure, but it might have something to do with her mouth tasting like a rhino cage and the fact that she just got up from sleeping on the pavement. A credibility issue, she thinks, although logic has never been her strong suit, either. It dawns on her as she sprints eastward across the lawns that there is north and south and west, all possible directions that Mason could have gone in. But why would he wander away? She doesn't know. She only knows the thud of her heart pounding wildly in her chest and mouth.

She stops running. She must calm down and do a systematic search. Contain the area. Think like a kid. Where would a kid go? How much ground could a nine-year-old cover? How much of a head start does he have on her? Could he have gotten frightened in the middle of the night and wanted to go home? It's forty blocks to home; surely he wouldn't try to go on his own, would he? And why wouldn't he wake her? Maybe he tried in his quiet, non-verbal way, but she was sleeping too soundly? No, it couldn't have been that. She had only four glasses of wine. She hoped it wasn't that.

She'd go in the direction of lights and movement and sound, she decides. That is, if she was a kid. She looks back down the street to where their fort is. No sign of anything. The dark is daunting and the trees' giant, crisscrossed fingers extending over the street look terrifying.

Not even on Broadway yet, and Beth realizes she doesn't have her Fluevogs on. A sharp stone informs her that in her panic she's been running in her white cotton sweat socks. But by the time she goes back and retrieves her Fluevogs from the fort where she was using them as a pillow, she will have wasted five full minutes. She decides it is more important that she make a full loop around Broadway before too much time has passed. Mason might only be two minutes ahead of her; she has no way of knowing. Time is a premium she can't afford to waste. Her sweat socks are Kodiaks, relatively thick as socks go.

On Broadway a few people are roaming around, mostly groups of college or UBC students. You can tell a student by their clothes, Beth thinks, although if questioned, she wouldn't know what the distinction would be. It could be the casual, confident way they dress as opposed to the actual clothing they wear. Whatever, she knows a student when she sees one. She stops and asks a young couple what time it is and have they seen a boy, a small boy built like a sparrow – about this height? She guesses Mason's height with her hand to be around four foot something. The girl looks at her digital watch. "It's

1:49," she says. As for the boy, no, neither of them has seen any boy of any height out this late. "Is he lost?' the girl asks, leaning toward her, perhaps out of concern. She glances down at Beth's sock feet. Beth feels her face reddening. "Not really, he's homeless," she says. The girl stares at her and noticeably pulls back. "Never mind," Beth says. She sprints off, checking out each juniper bush, every nook and cranny and darkened doorway that they checked out to begin with that Mason might have come back to and ducked inside. She's hissing his name out loud every four strides now. She looks back once and sees the couple standing where she left them, watching her.

As she jogs down Broadway in her stocking feet, her panic mounts. It would be one thing to lose your own child, as horrifying as that might be, but to lose someone else's is a nightmare that she may never recover from. Why, she thinks, why would he wander away? It's not the why that's important at the moment. Why is neither here nor there and that's the whole problem – neither here nor there. It's the where that matters. Beth realizes she is running so hard she can hardly breathe, let alone see where she's going. She slows down. She must keep her head about her and do a proper search. She knows this stuff; it's what she trained for in Search and Rescue. She knows about children hiding in small places because it makes them feel safe. She knows about children not responding to searchers because they are taught not to talk to strangers. She wishes she had her ready pack and the blue teddy she carries for exactly that reason in order to coax them out, win them over, gain their trust. She shudders for a moment at the thought that a child can be so easily swayed by a blue teddy. She's sure Mason wouldn't be, and wouldn't need any coaxing either, at least not from her. He's probably in the same ghastly nightmare she's in. She can't think about that now. She needs to stay focussed. With any luck, he's tucked himself into a comfortable box somewhere, something similar to their fort. If she can just stay calm, then everything will be all right. They'll be fine, she recalls thinking earlier as she studied Mason's sweet, fine-featured face while he slept. His tiny, perfect ears and soft child-cheeks. And they will be fine, again, she tells herself over and over like a mantra as she scours Broadway.

She goes past one of Vancouver's most elite restaurants. She glances in the window on her way by. You can tell these people by their shoes. Even though wealthy people might look like everyone else, it's their footwear that gives them away. Usually expensive slim Italian leather or designer shoes where the shoehorns themselves start at two hundred and fifty dollars. Ridiculous, Beth thinks. Perhaps she could start up an awareness program where she guides wealthy, shoeless people along Hastings Street in the early morning.

She sprints past the Salvation Army and crosses over to Benny's. Benny's is hopping with people now. Exactly what she needs. Some warm bodies to help her search for Mason. It's Saturday night, there's a good chance that Laurel and Gwen from Dairyland could be here. Beth pauses outside the window to catch her breath. She pulls her t-shirt down and pushes her bobbed hair behind her ears. She opens the doors and sees the 'No Shirt, No Shoes, No Service' sign. She glances around the room to see if anyone is looking, but everyone is otherwise engaged. Besides, she's only here to grab a few willing bodies and she'll be off before management notices. She looks down at her socks. They are black from the street and she thinks she has gum on the left one. She moves over to the counter where her feet will be less noticeable. The fresh-baked smell of bagels coming out of the clay oven greets her. All that running has made her hungry again.

She looks around the low-lit room. The place is jammed to the gunnels. Every chair and table, even the counters along the windows are filled with people laughing and drinking and smoking. Good god, she could use a cigarette right now. Even one drag would calm her nerves. She inhales the dark air deeply savouring the second-hand smoke. She's thankful for the dissidents in the crowd who choose to ignore Vancouver's stringent by-laws. Neither does the staff seem to care. She scans the crowd for the Saturday night regulars, faces she knows, not necessarily acquaintances, but not total strangers, either. She looks for Gwen or Laurel and thinks she spots Laurel at the back of the room chair-dancing at a table full of guys.

"Beth!"

Beth turns and sees Laurel and Gwen at a table by the front window. The table is littered with empty Sleeman bottles and the waitress juggles her tray of lox and cream cheese bagels and half a dozen water-coloured shooters in order to clear a space to put the baskets down. Finally the waitress hands the tray to Gwen and loads the empty beer bottles onto the counter behind them.

"Come, come." Gwen waves her over like she's landing an airplane.

Beth lands.

"Beth, we were just talking about you," Laurel says, loudly.

"All good things, I hope?" Beth asks back, stiffly. She always finds it initially awkward and unpleasant to run into a friend who's had a decent head start. She looks at Gwen. Gwen scrunches her eyes up and beams at her. Beth can see she's had a big head start – probably a five-hour head start, by the goofy expression on her face. Laurel slides a shooter across the table. Beth looks at it. Her mild hangover from White Spot has developed into a rhythmic booming ground on either side her temples – nothing that a handful of Tylenol 3s or an entire bottle of J.D. or finding a missing child wouldn't cure. She ignores the shooter. It's a mere drop in her ocean of horrors.

"Of course it's good. We fucking love you, Beth," Laurel shouts over the noise. Three guys next to them are having a chugging contest and half of Benny's is egging them on. Laurel's eyes are glassy and she's talking slower than normal. Gwen laughs wildly.

"Sit down and eat these with us." Laurel unfolds a wooden chair from against the wall.

"I came for help—" Beth says.

"What?" Gwen leans forward to hear and nearly falls out of her chair.

"Help, I said – help," Beth shouts. Gwen and Laurel look at her blankly. Gwen's eyes are swimming in her head and Laurel can't stop herself from grinning like it's a joke that Beth is about to spring on them.

"Here's all the help you need," Laurel says, pushing the shooter in front of her, but Laurel's not really paying attention. She's watching the chuggers; in particular, Beth thinks, the broad-shouldered one who looks like a swimmer and has the maple leaf shaved into the back of his head. He slams his empty bottle of Canadian down on the table and then raises both arms in triumph. The whole room erupts into a thunderous cheer. Beth's head is pounding and she can feel a cold fear moving up from her stomach. She needs help. She needs a posse, a search and rescue team. She needs capable bodies. She needs to quell her anxiety before she stands up and gets hysterical in the middle of the laughing and chugging and cheering. These people are of no use to her. She takes the shooter and drinks it in one neat shot. It burns warm and licorice down her throat. She gets up to go but Laurel grabs her by the arm and pulls her back down.

"Don't go, we need you," Laurel says, and divides the remaining shooters up between them. Gwen picks hers up and so does Laurel. The two of them wait for Beth.

"I have to go," Beth says and wants to explain further but it's the stupid smile plastered all over Laurel's face that stops her and Gwen is suddenly waving at two men standing at the front door. How can she tell Laurel and Gwen that she and a nine-year-old boy were sleeping on the street a few blocks down and now she's lost him? Laurel wouldn't understand and Gwen is beyond comprehension. They wait for her to pick up her shooter. What the fuck, she thinks; the ocean can't get any deeper. She picks up the shooter and the three of them slam them back. Laurel finishes first and bangs hers down on the table. She raises both arms up in the air. The maple leaf chugger laughs like hell and high-fives her.

"Who's that?" Beth asks, meaning the two men at the door. Men without chairs, she thinks, and then giddily, like the band, Men Without Hats. Her head is feeling better now, like cotton batten, the throbbing has rounded out to a dull ache with the second shooter. She is no longer a woman on the verge of a nervous breakdown. She's right back where she left off at White Spot, in a nebulous everything-will-be-fine fog. She takes a cigarette from Gwen's pack and lights it.

"Come, join us," Beth hears Gwen saying. She looks up to see a silver-haired man. He's slim and muscular like a college boy, like the maple leaf swimmer next to them. His face is pleasant, not overly handsome, but flawlessly smooth and blondish. The kind of face you see on dermatologists. Laurel unfolds two chairs for the men. Beth looks at the younger, second man. He looks like Brad Pitt, except with striking black hair about shoulder length. He could do commercials for Vidal Sassoon. Beth feels the weight of her dateless four months in her groin, along the surface of her skin, a strong tingling sensation that she remembers, out of the blue, like she's had sex and men yesterday.

Laurel and Gwen eye the younger friend, too. Beth

thinks he's probably the secret weapon that the older, silver-haired man uses in a pinch. If he can't get in on his own reconnaissance, then he pulls out the younger one to clinch the deal. Not that Beth or Laurel or Gwen would hold shabby candles to either of these men. They are all, if you happened into Benny's at this moment, a good-looking crowd. Beth notices that several tables turn and glance in the direction of the friend. The waitress comes over with two shooters, molasses-coloured this time.

"From the next table," she says. Laurel turns and high-fives the grinning swimmer. He takes a shooter from the tray and hands the other to Laurel. They clink glasses and drink. Laurel does the victory slam and the roar is massive. Beth gets up to leave. She has a sense of urgency, although it's heavy, like being buried under sand.

"What time is it?" she asks the silver-haired man.

"I don't know. I don't have a watch." He looks around the room and spots a neon pink bagel clock on the far wall.

"It's just after 2:00," he says.

The waitress comes with another tray of shooters

that Laurel must have ordered and Beth is forced to move over and finds herself arm to arm with the older man. Neither of them moves apart. Beth looks at him. His skin is exquisite, like Maple's but in a different, Ivory-soap sort of way. Perhaps it's skin she's truly looking for, skin to run your calloused palms over. She smiles. He smiles back.

Now that they are seated and the waitress off-loads ten shooters, they spend a few inarticulate moments checking each other out, doing some mental calculations as to who might go with whom, and if not, well, then, whomever will do. Certainly Brad Pitt is the number-one choice but second choice is no loss either. As for Laurel, Gwen and Beth herself, they are all in top form: ample women, older, yes, but in better shape than their younger counterparts because they are still shopping. They haven't locked into any long-term GICs (Guys In Condos) at this point in their lives. More important for all of them is their willingness. Not to mention childbirth and breastfeeding and the drudgery of child rearing haven't yet ravaged their bodies. Beth keeps glancing over at the beautiful facsimile of Brad Pitt. She wishes she were going to be there to get first-round draft pick. She could teach this youngster a thing or two. He is probably not as young as she thinks. Could be twenty-five, perhaps twenty-six. The older one is definitely more their age even though his hair has gone prematurely grey. Still, his body. There is something attractive about older, athletic men that Beth likes. You get top form and a person you can talk to as well.

Laurel places two shooters in front of each of them.

"Cheers to Dairyland," she says and raises her shot glass.

The older one, more refined and with practiced charisma, raises his shooter.

"Here's to granting Ken," he motions at Brad Pitt, "and myself, Sam, the pleasure of your company."

He looks directly at Beth. Beth blushes. Everyone has their shot glasses poised in the air waiting for her.

"I've really got to go," Beth says, but they are all staring at her.

"One for the road?" Sam asks.

Beth looks around the room. The lights are a soft yellow and everyone is talking and laughing. The chuggers are sharing a platter of nachos. The chair-dancing woman in the corner that Beth initially thought was

Laurel, is up now and vibrating around the room. The mother-scent of yeast is in the air, not at all like sea air or the wafting fatty odour of dirty bird from KFC. She steals a glance across the table at Brad, no, Ken, like a Totally-Hair-Ken doll, she thinks. He would be absolutely suited to a Barbie doll and/or girl. Then she remembers *Word on the Street* Kenneth and laughs hysterically.

"What's so funny?" Sam asks.

"Nothing," she says.

Sam looks dejected.

"Well, there's this guy, a homeless guy actually, that stands out in front of the Chinese grocery next door. Maybe you've seen him?" Beth asks.

Sam shakes his head. Laurel and Gwen and Ken are still waiting with their shooters in the air. Beth is fully aware that they are all listening carefully, but she's not sure she can explain what she finds so absurdly funny about the *Kenneth* coat on a homeless guy whose name isn't Kenneth at all. Yet here is the man of any woman's dreams sitting across the table from her and his name is Ken. Must be the contrast that makes it so funny, Beth thinks, but fears it may be lost on everyone except her.

That and the fact that she is supposed to be homeless at this very moment. They'd think she was batty.

"For the road," Beth says, lifting her shooter into the air, "literally." She downs her shooter and laughs again. Sam runs his hand across her arm as if to soothe her savage, hysterical beast. Beth squints at him in the yellow light and likes him – a lot. Let Gwen and Laurel fight over Ken-doll, she'd take this one any day. Too bad she has to go.

Or does she?

Oh, my god. Mason. She looks madly around for the neon clock. It's 2:45. She has to go. She's got an ordinary boy to find. Mason is out there, truly homeless and alone. She stands up quickly. Too quickly. Her head is woozy. She steadies herself on the counter. Sam stands up, also and gives her his arm for balance. She looks down and sees her once-white sweat socks, now dark and grey and blotchy with oil from her jaunt down Broadway. Yes, that is bubble gum on the left one. Great, she thinks, bubble gum is a bitch to get out. Sam looks down and sees them, too.

"Did you lose your shoes?" he asks.

What a question. If she lies and says, 'Funny you

should notice, but yes, I did lose my shoes on the way over here.' He will think she's a regular in the psych ward at St. Paul's. If she tells him the truth, then Gwen and Laurel will also find out and she'll be dairy cooler fodder for the next month at work. Like the guy at Dairyland that whacked off in the cooler of one of the Safeways he delivered to (strange, Beth thinks, why would you masturbate in a dairy cooler?). A four year-old-kid spotted him through the tubs of sour cream and yoghurt and told his grandmother. Last they heard the guy was working as an usher at the Pacific Coliseum. Seven-forty-eight an hour.

Beth looks around the table. Gwen is having a one-on-one conversation with Ken-doll. They are both leaning into the table, talking in low, serious voices. Laurel has gyrated like a stripper off Water Street over to the table next door with the chuggers. Apparently, like the woman pulsating around the room, Laurel is plugged into some higher place where the strobe lights are flashing and the music is a private rave for her and her chair and the broad-shouldered swimmer. Beth has to strain to hear the music over the noise of the crowd.

Sam puts his hand on the small of her back. The

exact spot that aches from having slept on the street. She relaxes into his hand for a brief moment. He tells Beth he's a plastic surgeon. Odd that he would tell he that now as she wavers unsteadily at the table and has to leave. Should she be impressed? Beth wonders if he does harelip reconstructions or works on burn patients? She hopes he doesn't specialize in boob jobs. But who knows, if in a decade from now, if she's still not married or residing with her life's partner, then perhaps a breast implant wouldn't hurt?

"Where are you going?" Sam asks. "Can I come, too?"

Beth looks at him. He's warm, he's capable, and more importantly, he's not drunk.

"I've got to go now," she says, looking desperate.

"No problem," Sam says, and shoots down both his and Beth's Sambucas back-to-back. Ken sees that they are leaving and takes a small white packet out of his pocket and slides it across the table to Sam. Sam winks at him. Gwen laughs once, loud like a shot and it startles the restaurant into a three-second hiatus. In the lull, Bath can hear Laurel's cadenced private rave from the speakers overhead. Sam skilfully slips his hand over the packet and tucks it into the breast pocket of his MEC coat. Mountain Equipment Co-op like their sleeping bags that got jacked, Beth thinks. Christ, Mason! She's got to go. She sees Ken tracing Gwen's lifeline well past her palm up her forearm to her collarbone and in the vicinity of her V-neck blouse as she lurches past Laurel at the next table. Sam follows her out.

Outside the air is cool and damp and it confuses her for a minute. Which way did she come from? Beth stops and looks both ways down Broadway.

"Forget where you live, too?" Sam smiles.

Beth decides that she came from *that* direction and starts to walk fast in her stocking feet.

"Whoa, whoa, I didn't bring my jogging shoes," Sam laughs, and beneath the tattered canopy of the Chinese grocers, he stops and pulls her in for a kiss. A warm, anise-liquory kiss.

"Care for a quick snort?" he asks, pulling Ken-doll's white packet from his coat.

"No, thank you," Beth says. "I had a problem with that at one time," she says, as if to imply that she may have been addicted to cocaine, when in actuality, she did it once for three days straight and then went to work at

Dairyland where she walked around with a hundred-and-six-degree fever and pneumonia for several weeks after. When she finally did go to the doctor, he found scar tissue on her right lung in the x-ray. She thinks there may be a correlation between the two.

"Do you mind?" he gestures with the cocaine.

"No, but I really have to leave."

She's frantic now that it's been too long, that she couldn't possibly find Mason after all this time. Unless he's found his way back to their fort and he's there right now wondering where she is. That thought calms her slightly. Everything will be all right. She draws a deep, yogic breath. She waits a moment while Sam scoops some coke up in a tiny silver spoon and snorts it. He sighs.

"I'm going to be awake all night now," he says. His eyes are bright in the dim light of the street lamp, and they are green. Deep enough green that Beth thinks she can tell him and he won't think she's off her rocker.

"I'm homeless," she says and laughs at the sound of that.

He laughs, too. Homeless is not normally a subject attached to humour. Beth looks closely at him. He looks a little terrified, she thinks. After all, she isn't wearing any shoes and her sweat socks are a disaster.

"Not really homeless but homeless for the night. We've got a fort on MacDonald—"

"We? There are more of you?" Sam asks. His eyes glitter.

"There's a boy a nine year-old boy and we had hamburgers and I had wine and we had a fort and there's a writer and our stuff got stolen and I do have a house and I fell asleep and he wasn't there when I woke up and I need help." Tears well up in her eyes and she can't stop them.

Sam puts his arms around her and she sobs into his nylon jacket. When she's done, he takes her by the shoulders and makes her look him in the eye.

"A boy? A nine year-old boy out there alone?" he asks.

Beth walks faster, watching the sidewalk for broken glass. She could use a cigarette, too. While she hadn't pegged Sam as a plastic surgeon (surely with that skin, you'd go into dermatology?) neither had she pegged him as someone who did cocaine. Or cared, for that matter. Most guys would have been long gone by now. But she's sure he's not a smoker. She scours the ground in the dark.

"You're staying in a tree fort?" Sam asks.

"Well, not quite but sort of," Beth says. "There's a writer that lives on the block." She doesn't fully comprehend what the writer has to do with anything except, perhaps, to lull her into a peculiar kind of comfort that *he* has a social conscience, even if hers is a little shaky. She lets Sam think what he will.

One block down Broadway and Beth cuts up to MacDonald. She's sure it's only another block or so. Or was that from the White Spot? She checks up and down the dark suburban lane covered in trees. "Are those chestnuts or maples?" she asks Sam.

"I can't tell," Sam says, squinting into the blackness. "Where's the fort? Who is the writer, anyone I might know? I've been to a few readings myself. Is the boy alone now?" Sam wants to know. Beth wanders down the block. The trees are massive and they all look the same. She couldn't tell a maple from a chestnut even in full sun. She feels groggy and disoriented. What she'd like to do is sink down and fall asleep in the rhododendron bushes, or go home and catch a rerun of Hawaii Five-O in the shelter of her own home, but Mason is at the forefront of her sluggish mind and she knows that come high tide or morning, if she can't locate their fort, she's got a life-altering misdemeanor on her hands and she really will need a tent.

"Give me some of that," she says to Sam. "I can't think straight."

Sam laughs at the logic of that, although he seems sharper, more alert, less drunk than he did when they first started out. He takes the folded paper from his breast pocket and offers her the spoon.

"You don't have any cigarettes, do you?"

It so happens he does, solely for the purpose of chance and choice. If you can't find a secure place to spoon, then the least you can do is dip a government-approved substance in an illegal one and hope that no one around you recognizes the bitter odour of burning cocaine. He smokes it in restaurants, he says, when, with a proper tip, he can get away with it. Even that elite one they just passed on Broadway.

Beth looks down at his shoes. Sure enough they are slim-soled, Italian leather. Now she's sure about wanting Sam to come to their fort.

She lights the cigarette and inhales deeply, audibly. She feels a slight twinge in her right lung and thinks she'd better stop, but the cigarette and cocaine taste so good on top of the licorice liquor and the ghost of anyone's lips that she has been so long without. She allows herself a dip or two more.

Beth sees the glassy look in Sam's eyes and tries to focus more clearly in the damp night. Sam seems to be watching her with genuine concern. He's no longer a man with a mission to get laid. Perhaps she's underestimated him? She shivers. She wishes she'd worn her fleece. What did she do with her fleece, anyway? She was sure she had it on earlier. And shoes, she had those, too. Didn't she? The cocaine makes the night air seem thicker, porous like drizzle. Warm is the goal, she thinks. She remembers vaguely a joke that if the situation gets tough, then she'll go out and rustle up a *Vancouver Sun* to cover up with. She can't remember whom she told it to, but it's not a bad idea. She thinks about asking Sam for either his coat or his shoes. Share the wealth, she thinks, but doesn't have the wherewithal to ask anything of anyone who is good enough to follow a shoeless woman around in the dark long after the prospect of sex has vanished. She wishes she knew what time it was. She stops and listens for the distant tide, the strumming guitar. She hears neither, which means that she is either way off base as to where their fort is, or else everyone has left Jericho Beach and the ocean has stopped rolling up onto the sand. She starts to hum beneath her breath.

"Let it be, let it be," Sam recognizes the song and sings. "Speaking words of wisdom, let it be."

Speaking words of wisdom, Beth looks up at him. She takes his hand and they walk along the side streets softly singing Paul McCartney. Up ahead, Beth sees the blockade of signs and the dark silhouette of the Perego double stroller. She cries out into the still air.

"Our fort!" she says. She yells Mason's name out full throttle. Sam jumps.

She sprints the half block and vaults the blockade like a hurtle racer. She feels the slowness of her forward pitch, like watching a track-and-field recap on TV. Her right leg straightens and sails over the blockade at the same time her upper body folds proficiently to manage the height and just when she thinks she's got it, the heel of her back foot catches on the top of the No Exit sign. She and the sign crash down. The last thing she remembers is the hard, unforgiving asphalt against her soft cheek.

Sam runs over, alarmed, and finds Beth lying face-first. He presses his way into the square of signs and kneels down. She's not moving but she's breathing. He pushes his hands under her prone body to check for bleeding, and as he does, his wrist skims the surface of her breast. Real, he thinks. A real woman with real breasts, how refreshing. Then he lifts her head ever so slightly to avoid neck injury and cups her head in his hands to check for bumps. She's clean. Unconscious but not in danger of bleeding to death on MacDonald street. Her left cheek is scraped up pretty good. He takes out a Kleenex and blots her cheek. The Kleenex sticks and he leaves it there.

Sam does a hasty search of the fort and can't find

anything but a pair of shoes on the pavement. Fluevogs – nice Fluevogs. Olive swirls; real leather; thick, Satan-resistant soles. He's wandered by the store on Granville and seen the signs, but has never gone inside. He might have to check it out after all. There's a twisted-up metal chair of some kind, no doubt abandoned by some neighbour who didn't want to haul it over to the dump. Jackass, he thinks. He takes his coat off and lifts one of Beth's arms above her head and rolls her onto her side and then onto his coat, which he zips up for warmth. She's in need of some medical help. He looks at the four houses on the corner, trying to decide which one is the writer that Beth knows. He can't very well go ringing doorbells indiscriminately at this hour of the morning. And he doesn't carry a cell phone. There's hardly a need to perform emergency breast implants and really, when that goes out of Vogue and skinny-chested women come back in, he may have to go back to doing cleft palates, which was what he was trained for in the first place. A lot less money, but worthy of a cell phone, he thinks.

If he hurries he can make it down to Benny's to catch Beth's friends. Maybe they will have some insight into this fort business and the no shoes and the boy. And Ken. Ken has his car there. Perhaps this happens to Beth all the time. She gets drunk and forgets where she left her shoes, then knocks herself out. He hates to call an ambulance if it's not warranted. What does he know? He just met her. Surely she'll be all right in the amount of time it will take him to sprint down to Benny's.

Beth comes to and struggles to sit up, but she can't because she's got her arms ludicrously on the inside of her coat and the zipper is done up to her chin. It's like a straitjacket. She manages to turn onto her side and press her face on the asphalt to work herself up into a sitting position. Where the hell is she? She looks at the clutter of signs and remembers that she is homeless this long weekend. Her tongue tingles numbly, tastes powdery and acrid, and she remembers she is homeless, but on a cocaine budget. Lucky her. She hopes her lung will not start to ache. Her head certainly does, and her feet feel like she's run a 10K in bare feet. She touches her face. There's a Kleenex stuck to her cheek and when she tries to pull it off, it stings. She leaves it there. The coat she's wearing is not her own. But whose is it? It's one of those Mountain Equipment Co-op cycling coats with the fluorescent strips down the front and sides. Then she remembers Mason. Oh, my God, Mason! Where is he? Did she take him home after White Spot before she went to Benny's? She recalls White Spot. At least the Madonna waitress comes to mind, and vaguely that she ordered two beef-patty burgers with fries and bovine gravy. How could she forget that? And sundaes chock full of Dairyland. Maple – unrequited-love-of-her-life – Maple will never forgive her for that. What else did she forget?

She looks over at her pair of Fluevog shoes, oddly not on her feet but lying on the dark street like someone forgot to put them in the front hall closet. Then she sees the aluminum hammock-shaped chair that she *knows* a nine-year-old boy had been sleeping on earlier. She struggles the zipper down on the cycling coat and pushes her arms into the sleeves. She feels something firm in the breast pocket on the inside. She pulls it out. She doesn't have to open the folded paper to know what it is. She gets up and kicks over the Danger! sign.

She runs down the shadowy street calling Mason's name as loud as she can. A few house lights come on after she's turned the corner to go up Cypress to Maple.

Sam bursts into Benny's and finds Beth's friend, the loud one, showing a table of young guys her newly pierced belly button. Makes her seem less like their mothers, who plausibly she could be if she'd had a baby in grade twelve, which is the age these guys look. Sam is not sure they are even old enough to be drinking beer, let alone gazing at an older woman's silver-studded umbilical cord when their own have been clipped less than two decades ago. Sam rushes over to the table and grabs her by the arm. He doesn't see Ken or Gwen. They must have left.

"Betty," he says.

Laurel stares at him. She can't place him, nor does she know anyone named Betty.

One of her offspring stands up. He's got a maple leaf shaved into his hair and is tall. He looms above Sam's silver hair. Sam feels like Mrs. Robinson's husband come to wretch her away from seducing school-age boys.

"Beth, she's—" he says, out of breath. She's fallen and she can't get up is what he wants to say, but it comes out in a rushed slur: "Shuvallungungunup."

"Oh, Beth!" Laurel says. She understands the language of the intoxicated. She pats the tall boy on his broad swimmer's shoulder and he sits down obediently.

Sam takes a deep breath. "Have you got a car?" he asks.

Laurel waves a full shot glass at him and says she can't go until – Sam takes the glass and shoots it back.

"Okay, let's go," he says.

Laurel looks offended. She meant it as a game of sipping seduction where the three boys at the table all have a few extra minutes to rock/paper/scissor telepathically among themselves as to who's going to get busy with her. All three look disappointed when Sam hauls Laurel up and throws her purse over her shoulder. Sam leads her out of Benny's and Laurel staggers over to where her Jeep is parked. Laurel decides she should drive because it's hers and it's brand new and it's a standard and she doesn't think her insurance will cover another driver and — Sam wrestles the keys from her and manages to get her into the passenger seat. Laurel slumps back on the seat and her head lolls against the window. Sam lurches forward and drives down Broadway shifting straight from second to fourth gear. Laurel opens the window and throws up down the side of her copper-coloured Jeep. When she pulls herself back in, the Jeep reeks of vomit but Laurel is almost sober.

"Where's Beth?" she asks, wiping her sticky mouth on her short sleeve.

"She's homeless. She jumped over some signs and fell and knocked herself out. Has she ever done this before?" Sam asks.

"What? Been homeless or knocked herself out?" Laurel may be drunk, but she's sharp.

"Either," says Sam.

"Not that I know of. She owns a house not far from here and as far as knocking herself out, she only does that when there's someone worth impressing," Laurel smiles in the fuzzy dark. A line of lime-coloured light is starting on the eastern horizon.

"Does she have kids?" Sam asks, "A boy?"

"Not tonight," Laurel says.

Sam turns down MacDonald and drives up a couple blocks until he comes to the barricade of signs. He stops, leaves the headlights on, and gets out and disappears into the middle of the signs. Laurel gets out and staggers over to the rhododendron bushes and throws up again.

She comes and peers over the signs. Sam is checking the ground with his hands. All he can find are the shoes and the bent aluminum chair.

"She still homeless?" Laurel asks.

"Look," Sam says. He shows Laurel the Fluevogs.

Laurel squints in the strained light of dawn.

"Those are Beth's! Where is she?" Laurel asks, her eyes narrowing as if Sam has done something to her friend and now he's lured her out here also. Laurel stands up as tall as she can. Sam is a good six inches taller but his wrists are almost feminine in their fineness.

"Oh, for Christ's sake," Sam says, seeing Laurel puff herself out defensively, "I haven't done anything to her. She was here and I came to get you to take her home."

They both look around. The sun is peeking down at the beach now, throwing a gold sheen on the tree-lined street.

Beth's mind meanders as she wanders the streets. Her voice is hoarse and dry from calling, and the dawn air is cold and damp and the numbness has worn away from her tongue and gone into her tired brain. She wills herself up and down the streets named after trees named after Mason's mother, checking each cross-avenue, calling out Mason's name then waiting fifteen seconds for his response that she knows she won't get because no one is there to interpret for him. She's sick in the pit of her stomach and her right lung hurts and she forgot her shoes twice in one night. Her socks are black with the street, and wet, and there's a hole in the left one where the bubble gum has worn away. She's done with homeless, boyless, aloneness. She wishes someone would come along and take her in their capable arms and tell her everything is going to be all right. She wishes someone would come along and buy her a steaming grande low fat latte or organize a search party and let her sleep in their unheated garage until this was all over.

She ends up out on Broadway again and this time in her fatigue sits down on the curb and rubs her cold hands together. The sleeves of the coat hang down several inches past her hands and she notices the breast pocket's been embroidered, not with a MEC logo but with a name. *Sam*, it says. She bursts out laughing at the oversized coat, the name that's not hers but Sam's. She remembers Sam now, with the silver hair and athletic twenty-year-old body. Sam with anise lips and slim Italian leather shoes and cocaine and cigarettes and warm hands and charitable enough to walk a shoeless woman back to her fort in the middle of the street and believe her when she says she owns Fluevogs and a house and had a boy. Sam would wrap his arms around her and buy her a Starbucks for her distant numb head and round up a posse to look for Mason. She feels herself warming to the idea of children in general, especially strange, awkward, intelligent children. She throws her head back and laughs with the abandon of a sleeping child. The first jogger of the morning runs by and cuts a wide swath around her on the sidewalk. Beth laughs at that, too, at the idea that the jogger thinks she's homeless and possibly dangerous. She laughs until tears come to her eyes, and then she sobs.

Sam drives up and down the streets in Laurel's Jeep. Laurel is asleep in the passenger seat, snoring. After laying her hand on Sam's thigh but then having it removed by Sam like a wet, sour dishrag, she must have decided that sleep was the next best option. Sam looks down the streets, checking out any shrub large enough to house a full-grown woman and possibly a nine-year-old boy, if Beth is to be believed. And he thinks she is believable even though she wasn't wearing any shoes. If shoes define the man (as he knows from his own thin Italian leather ones) then what do sweat socks say about the woman? But Beth didn't seem off her rocker, just pleasantly unhinged. She said she owned her own house not far from Benny's. He'd heard that some homeless people did have apartments or boarding houses where they lived, they just had some major problems that prevented them from getting home every night. Like three-week benders in the back of abandoned station wagons because the liquor store was close by and you could always find a buddy in as much need of a stiff drink of cheap bourbon and Lysol-sprayed bread as you. The company of strangers is preferable to the company of none, Sam thinks as he searches the sidewalks and yards for Beth and, yes, the boy. Hell, as shoeless people go, Beth is as genuine and real as any slim-soled-shoeful women that he has come across lately. He can't stop thinking about her breasts. The genuine article. Almost inspirational.

Maple is tight on the verge of candid hysteria, her skin no longer smooth and syrupy and beautiful but aged suddenly, as if fifty years walks in off the street when Beth shows up at the door and Mason isn't with her. Carl is the colour of feud blood as he calls the Vancouver police to report his only child missing. Neither one asks Beth in and she stands at the brightly painted turquoise oak door on Balsam Street ill-at-ease in her large MEC coat with some man's name embroidered on it, a gram of another man's cocaine in her left pocket, an ache in her right lung, her heart and belly, and black sweat socks stretched clownishly in size and shape. Maple won't look her in the eye. Carl can't stop staring at her in horror, but it is Maple's aversion that makes Beth want to lie down on the floor in the fetal position and beg for forgiveness.

Or perhaps, Beth thinks as she sobs on the curb on Broadway in broad daylight envisioning Maple and Carl's reaction, perhaps it would be better to still look for Mason on her own? If she can find him, then she won't be forced to stand in Maple and Carl's doorway and tell them that she has inadvertently lost their son. And perhaps, too, Mason would not be so predisposed to blurting it all out. If she can find Mason first, she can take him to McDonald's or worse, KFC as his reward for being homeless. Where can he be? Where could he have gone? It occurs to Beth in an icy rush of fear up her spine that someone or something came along and happened to Mason while she was sleeping. Rather, she'd like to think he woke up, got bored or scared or had to go to the bathroom, the latter, probably, and wandered off. He may have gotten disoriented by the trees and the dark and couldn't make his way back to their fort. He, like any kid, would almost certainly head for the lights on Broadway. Or home? Maybe he was trying to go home. But forty blocks to home? What if he's at home this very minute and Maple is livid and Carl has called the Vancouver Police not to report a missing person but to commence the wo/manhunt on her person?

Wouldn't Beth be better off to show up at Maple's door and take what comes?

People are moving down Broadway: joggers, women in careful dresses, men in casual suits, all of them in Nike/Adidas footwear because they walk to work in the morning. Beth notices they veer around her on the curb. She doesn't mind anymore, she'd veer around herself if she could. Her brown streaked hair is tousled like she's had a wild night of sex instead of a wild night of being knocked out cold on MacDonald Street. She puts her hand to her cheek and realizes she still has the Kleenex attached to the side of her face. She rips it off. It's bright yellow.

MacDonald Street! The writer! The writer on MacDonald Street. Surely if anyone saw anything, it would be the writer. Possibly he saw where Mason wandered off.

Beth gets up and jogs as best she can in her sloppy socks and sore feet through the working crowd down to MacDonald Street.

A one-in-four chance. Four corners, four houses, one writer. She studies each one, and decides the writer's house is the one with the rhododendron bushes and fenced-in backyard. Beauty and privacy would be highly valued by a writer, she thinks. Why, she doesn't know. Just a gut feeling alongside the nausea in her stomach and the faint smell of vomit in the morning air that she can't quite locate. She looks up at the sun. It must be about 8:00. Early, yes, but not too early, she thinks, to walk up to a stranger's house and inquire if they've seen the whereabouts of a nine-year-old boy sleeping in amongst the construction signs out front of their residence. As she mounts the carpeted wood stairs, a City of Vancouver truck pulls up and four guys get out and stand around drinking coffee. Holy Mother of God! Working on a Sunday on the May long weekend? Why, they must be clocking in at double time and a half. Conceivably, these guys could be making fifty-five bucks an hour to stand around a hole in the middle of the street watching not only each other, but checking her out as well. Or so Beth imagines them, giving her an approving once-over, but when she turns and tucks her chin-length hair behind her ears she realizes they are staring at her like she's an apparition – one without shoes. She stares back at them; they go back to their coffee.

Beth rings the bell, waits. She rings the bell again. Behind her the city workers are making moves to commence work once the coffee break is done. Work starts at eight but work doesn't really start until the first Styrofoam cup of coffee is ingested. The front door opens. It's a beardless man with glasses and thick russet hair, looking nothing at all like a man of social conscience, let alone a writer. They are all bearded or bald or abnormal-looking, aren't they? This man could grace the aisle of any Safeway and be right at home. She fears the odds are against her and she will have to explain her ludicrous situation not once but twice, perhaps three times, even four if she's really off. She can't bear the thought of it. She thinks now that she should have chosen the house with the Perego double stroller in it, the least likely.

"Good morning," the man says, taking her all in with his easy brown eyes. The humiliation of no shoes burns in Beth's eyes but the fact that her socks are filthy burns brighter. What a stupid simple thing to be ashamed of, she thinks. So what? What can he tell about her? So she has no shoes. What does that make her? Homeless? Deranged? Poor? There is no real disgrace in that, she thinks. She stands taller and looks the man in the eye.

"I've lost a boy," she says, "I'm wondering if you've seen him?"

"When?" the man asks.

My whole life, Beth wants to answer.

"Last night – this morning. Late," she says.

"Was he wearing a hoodie?" the man asks.

"Yes!" Beth wants to jump up and throw her arms around the man's beardless neck.

"I saw a boy much earlier when I was working at my computer." The man gestures behind him to the computer in the living room. The window faces the front street. "But he wasn't alone."

Beth's skin jumps for her.

"He was with a man, medium build, had a beard, I suppose. They were out walking. Strange, I thought, for that time of night."

"When? When did you see them?" Beth asks.

"Around one, one-thirty, I think."

"What were you doing up at that time?" Beth asks.

"Writing," the man says.

Beth looks at the man again and decides that his hair

and soft eyes aren't so Safeway or conventional. He looks as if he might understand much more than meets her red-rimmed eyes. He also looks like the sort of man who does not make judgement calls either, and he has travelled to third-world countries where no doubt, he's seen much, much worse. She tells him her story. And while he does look intrigued, as Beth had anticipated, he also looks a little wary, not inclined, perhaps, to invite her in for a cup of hot coffee. Nor does he offer to round up the posse and he has no garage. He's got his own boy to get ready for baseball, he says. He nods his head and says vaguely, "Well then, good luck with that."

As if she's bought a raffle ticket and has no chance in hell of winning. He shuts the door and she hears the deadbolt click into place.

Beth flaps down the steps and stands a moment looking up and down the street. The city workers are below ground level now, probably playing cards. She thinks she can feel the writer's brown eyes squarely on her back and when she turns around to check, she's right. He's sitting at his computer, gazing out the front window, not necessarily at her but past her. As if she's suddenly invisible. As if the fact that having no shoes makes her less of a person. And suddenly her cheeks grow hot with indignation and beyond her long sleepless night, where she didn't even get to grace the asphalt with her soft cheek other than when she was unconscious, which of course she has no recollection of save for the bright yellow Kleenex (whose?) and scraped skin on her left cheek, she's spent the last four hours scouring the streets and shouting Mason's name until her voice went hoarse. She has every right to look the way she does. Then she remembers her Fluevogs and walks over to the construction site to look for them. They are nowhere to be found, but the bent aluminum chair has been tossed to one side and she tucks it under her arm. It may be all she has left, but damn it, it's hers. She glances at the Perego double stroller as she goes by, considers borrowing it until she can track down Mason but the writer has his eyes fixed firmly in her vicinity. She struts, hair mashed, head high, feet sore, around the corner and back up to Broadway.

The guy that is truly homeless stands in the morning,

only retiring to his fold-out chair with the American flag on it after lunch when he gets tired. Not that he's particularly old or has much in the way of patriotism to any country, but the Kenneth coat, the cane, and the chair were all cheap at the Salvation Army. You take what you can get. Kenneth hauls these three items everywhere he goes in a shopping cart he hijacked from Zeller's. The carts there are smaller, more manageable, and easier to manoeuvre up and down sidewalk curbs not intended for the handicapped. He stashes his prize cart behind the Chinese grocer's while he sells newspapers out front.

Kenneth holds *Word on the Street*, tilting the thin newspaper this way and that in the direction of each new passer-byer so they can better see the front-page picture. It's him! Kenneth is on the cover. "Seller of The Year," the headline reads. *Time Magazine's* . . . Man of the Year. *Vanity Fair's* . . . Face of the Month. His! Most of the passer-byers ignore him but a few stop and hand him a loonie in exchange for this week's issue of *Seller of the Year*. A good man with a good beard in a good picture, he thinks, but no one seems to register that the photo and seller are one and the same. Like those

Missing Children posters that you glance at in the mall and then promptly walk by the little boy who's been purposely planted to see how many people actually pay attention to those posters. He saw it on Oprah once at the men's shelter. They placed posters of a missing boy at all the entrances into the mall and then the boy who was dressed exactly as he was in the photo sat in the middle of the food fair in plain sight. No one – not one single person – pegged him as the missing boy on the poster. People are too busy to pay attention, Kenneth thinks. He leans down and winks at the boy in the hoodie, the boy who latched onto him on MacDonald Street earlier this morning with not so much as a poster or a mall to confirm or deny his missingness. Nor does the boy speak. Not unusual, Kenneth thinks. The boy has never been much of a talker. This he knows from the past year of brown-bag lunches the boy brings him every morning, Monday to Friday, and leaves beside his large Styrofoam box that before it housed him housed a brand new Kenmore Water Heater for the school.

The boy is devouring a Hostess Twinkie, the kind with the pink sponge cake covered in white coconut, and it must be good because he doesn't stop eating until it's gone. He looks up at Kenneth from beneath his hood and smiles. Kenneth hauls another squashed package out of his coat pocket and gives it to the boy. This one is chocolate with cream filling. The boy finishes it in about four seconds, then chases it down with a half can of Coke that Kenneth found on his way down from Kerrisdale.

Beth is tired of holding her head up higher than everyone else's to make up for her sock feet. She's tired of indignant, she's tired of people who make asinine assumptions, and from the looks of everyone she's passed this morning, they are all self-righteous idiots. If she could lie down for a few minutes, she could regain herself. She sits down in the doorway of a Bulk Foods store that doesn't open until 10:00. She looks around. Most of the other shops are still closed; surely she could have a thirty-minute snooze and be up and gone before anyone comes to open the shop? She leans her head against the brick wall of the building. A man comes out of nowhere inside the closed shop and raps the window sharply with an orange plastic scoop. He glares at her. Beth hauls herself up and walks down the street to the alleyway. It's Sunday, not garbage day, she can grab a few winks. She slides down next to a blue bin; the stench is faint still because it's morning and the heat hasn't set in yet to release the full disgusting odour of rotting fruits and vegetables from the Chinese grocer's out front. A few minutes. If she can close her eyes for a few solid minutes, she can get her bearings.

A silver-haired man in good leather shoes gets out of a Jeep in front of Benny's. Kenneth notices his shoes, because when his head is not otherwise hidden behind *Word on the Street* it is habitually tilted groundwise. Years of practice that he can't rid himself of. The homies, Kenneth calls them, are always looking up and outward as if to better see what they can conquer, much like their earlier counterparts, Columbus and Genghis Khan, while Kenneth seeks out the ground like the Indigenous before him even though he'd be as Caucasian as Cream of Wheat given a proper night's sleep and a week's worth of solid bathing. But it's as if his deliverance lies there. And it does. A leftover cigarette butt, dropped change, a half-eaten burger to tide him over until the men's shelter reopens at 5:00 for dinner, that single lost wedding ring he pawned last year at the Brokers on Main located conveniently next to the men's shelter. Of course Kenneth could pinch a loonie or two and buy a decent bagel lunch at Benny's but Kenneth is proud to represent *Word on the Street* and moreover he certainly wouldn't be Seller of the Year if he were dipping into the profits. No, Kenneth searches for what everyone else has overlooked. The simple things – the free and easy life on the street. Too bad there wasn't a women's shelter nearby, then he'd have no reason to stray further into the depths of Water Street in downtown Vancouver.

The leather-shoed man hands Kenneth a toonie, a dollar more than is necessary, but when Kenneth tries to hand the man his change, the man says no, he doesn't want the change, but then the man stands a moment longer. Kenneth raises his head and the man looks him squarely in the eye, something most people don't do.

"You haven't seen a woman, have you?" the man asks Kenneth. Kenneth glances sideways and sees a woman standing by Benny's. She looks pale and worn out, a little green around the gills.

"There's one there," Kenneth says.

"No," the man says, "that's just Laurel."

Kenneth stares at the silver-haired man. Sam realizes he must sound ludicrous. How can Sam explain to a homeless man that the woman he met last night was wonderful, breathtaking even now that morning has shed its limey-light on everything, and that she was homeless, well, not in point of fact, because she owns a home not far from here, but she *was* homeless last night and now he needs to find her. Sam is afraid the whole story may come out sounding patronizing, like he and the woman are so full of themselves that they have nothing better to do than play at being homeless. After all, homeless is what this guy does for a living. How can Sam explain properly so the man won't take offence? He doesn't bother.

Sam notices the edges of the canopy above the Chinese grocer's appear unnaturally bright, as if lined with neon instead of the tattered khaki canvas that in the real light of any other day looks shoddy and dilapidated. Even humankind seems larger this morning, too. Most likely, Sam thinks, because of *her* — homeless, shoeless Beth. Or perhaps he may have overdone the cocaine a bit and he hasn't had any sleep, so that suddenly, standing out on the street in his expensive Italian shoes, he feels displaced, like an exclusive fish out in the public waters. Homeless even. He feels an affinity with – with – and here Sam looks closer at the bearded seller and sees the name embroidered on the coat. Kenneth.

"Kenneth," Sam says and extends his hand, "it is a delight to meet you."

Kenneth looks at him with his intense blue eyes and tells Sam that Kenneth isn't his name. He doesn't bother to explain further. He shakes hands with Sam. He's happy for the moment to be addressed by a name. Any name. If anything, this coat has made him visible, a patron of the street, mankind's client, and friend even to the boy in the hoodie beside him. What does it matter if it's the right name or not?

Sam glances at the newspaper.

"Well, congratulations anyway," Sam says in reference to the front-page photo, "A handsome picture."

Kenneth beams like a new appliance. The boy in the hoodie steals a quick glance at Sam and then recedes back beneath his hood. Sam studies the boy carefully, but then decides by the bird-like size of the boy that he could only be five, six tops. He has no way of telling how tall the seated boy is, either. Certainly not nine years old. Certainly not the son of a scientist, or whatever Beth said the boy's mother was. He looks dishevelled and has a fleece on that's obviously not his. No, Sam thinks. This is not the boy he's looking for. He's probably son of Kenneth, the next heir to the Seller of the Year throne. Sad, Sam thinks, although the boy's health looks well enough. Skinny, though, but he doesn't seem overly traumatized, if one were to believe anything that can be detected by the naked eye. Without a psychiatrist or a microscope. Believing is seeing, isn't it?

Sam remembers he has a pair of shoes tucked beneath his arm. He didn't know what he was thinking when he grabbed Beth's Fluevogs from Laurel's lap in the Jeep and tucked them under his arm to ask the homeless man if he'd seen a fellow homeless woman. But that's just it, he wasn't thinking for once, *just being*, and the shoes seem necessary in finding Beth. He notes, not without irony, that he has not one but both shoes. For the love of God, he has her shoes! Surely then the smallest amount of effort would be to find her and at least return her shoes? Bare minimum would require that? He finds himself thinking about his wrist brushing over the beautiful smooth arc of Beth's natural breast. He looks down at his wrist. His blue veins are visible beneath the pale thin skin along with arteries and tendons and fine bones. Yes, the wrist is the most vulnerable of body parts, he thinks. What your mother used to gauge your health by, putting her wrist to your forehead, or the nurse taking your pulse. The wrist knows, he thinks. Possibly Beth is a woman whose mind he could admire? He glances over at Laurel who is standing in front of Benny's looking like hell, like the best cure for a hangover is to start back in before the headache settles around your temples. She's looking longingly through the window into Benny's.

"Why don't you get him to try the shoes on?" Laurel says and laughs like it's the funniest thing anyone's ever said.

"Ha, ha," Sam says, and thanks Kenneth, who doesn't bother to protest again that Kenneth is not his name. Sam sneaks another look at the young boy. He reaches out to chuck the boy's chin affectionately, but the boy flinches back. Sam gathers himself and the shoes and Laurel and they climb back into the Jeep.

In the alley next to the blue bin Beth sets the mangled aluminum chair down and then lies down beside it. She pulls the chair closer, as if for protection or weapon, should she be forced to wake up suddenly from her intended fifteen-minute shut-eye and defend either her person or personal property. She can smell stale beer coming from a pallet of empty Sleeman's and Pilsner and *I Am Canadian* – a nation that defines itself by its beer drinking. She realizes she must be directly behind Benny's, about a block away from her own home. She considers going home, but she can't with Mason still out there, homeless for real now while she went home and passed out on her parsley-coloured paisley-print sofa from Urban Barn. Mason's name is like a blinking billboard at the forefront of her throbbing hangover from last night's cocaine and however many shooters she ended up having. If she can grab a quick nap then she'll be up and Eve on the quest for the boy.

Alcohol is the sleep elixir of the homeless, she thinks as she struggles to find a comfortable position on the paved alley. It's not like she knows too many homeless people personally, but those she has observed regularly on her weekly milk deliveries (Kenneth being the exception now that he's gainfully employed) don't seem to be abstaining from anything that comes their way, legal or not, whether from the baking aisle of Safeway (vanilla) or the cleaning aisle (Lysol). If forced to make a choice, she'd definitely have gone for a few more shooters last night. It's what allows you to lie your soft cheek down on the coarse asphalt of any street. Or alley, she thinks. But as soon as her cheek hits the tarmac, *She Is Canadian* and drops down into her exhaustion like a felled tree.

Mabel hasn't aged fifty years but only one night. One long, mostly sleepless night. She hollers to Carl, who is in the back bedroom, which has been converted into an office, that she's going to take the car down to Broadway, pick up a few things, and walk around and see if she can find Mason and Beth. She's concerned that it's almost 10:00 AM and they are not back yet, but Beth's perpetual admiration for her – bordering, Mabel suspects at times, on actual love – quells her mother-nerves. Beth would not let anything happen to her Mason. She imagines them having breakfast somewhere, perhaps at Buddha's Belly on West Fourth where Mason likes to eat. He likes that orange-haired woman's nose ring. Oh, well, there are worse things than nose rings to worry about, like noise pollution and ozone depletion and a possible drought on the Prairie provinces that could impact the entire nation. Even beautiful British Columbia.

She lifts various piles of clothing and wads of paper searching for her wallet. Mabel wonders how their night went. If Mason got any sleep? If they had any excitement? She hopes at least on some level, that Mason found the whole experience stimulating, if not a little bit fun. He so rarely lets loose and has fun, Mabel thinks. Perhaps it was like camping out at an amusement park closed for the night. All the carousel tigers and lions and jumping dolphins and rides shut down, the night sky settling in on Mason and Beth like a blanket of hospitable constellations. The sounds of the street receding into the calm of the drifting tide. Sounds like something Mabel could use about now.

Mabel gets into the car and drives the forty blocks to Broadway. She parks in the lot behind Benny's because she knows they never check to see if people are inside buying bagels or not. She gathers her recycled hemp shopping bags, the current David Suzuki book she's reading, and her plastic wallet. From the passenger window, she sees someone sleeping next to the blue bin on the other side of the car. Mabel looks to see if she has any food in the car, anything that she might leave as an offering, a small token of her goodwill on behalf of both herself and the planet, and her son Mason who has spent the night (successfully, she hopes) on the street, like this unfortunate person no doubt has.

Mabel can't tell whether the slumbering figure is male or female. In the back of the car beneath a stack of newspapers that she's got to get to the recycling depot one of these days, she finds a can of guava juice. Warm from having been in the car for who knows how long, probably the last time she and Mason went to Stanley Park to see the howler monkeys, which was – when?

Last fall? She checks for an expiry date but can't find one, so she shuts the car door gently, so as not to wake the homeless from a well-deserved sleep. Then she tiptoes across the black pavement and sets the warm can of guava juice down beside the sleeping figure. She almost trips on a lawn chair.

A woman, Mabel guesses, seeing the tangle of stylishly cropped brown hair. The woman's face is hidden beneath her arms. The hair has streaks of blonde running through it like it's been professionally highlighted, or possibly the sleeping woman highlighted it herself? Mabel can't envision the woman sitting in the back alley, her head full of foils and peroxide, next to the blue bin with a crowd of scavenging ravens flapping about. It's probably natural, or from the abnormal amount of sun you would take in from always being on the street. And apart from the deprivation of living on the streets, the woman has no shoes either. Only a pair of filthy blackened socks. The left one has a hole in it, too. Mabel looks down at her own feet. Nice feet, if she does think so herself, a little guiltily. Slender, with toenails painted French white with blue and yellow daisies beneath her pink plastic sandals that are made entirely from recycled pop bottles. Clear and pink and sturdy. Exactly what someone on the street needs – this someone, this sleeping woman needs a robust pair of sandals to get around in. Mabel takes off her recycled sandals and feels the heat of the paved alley on her feet. Something she hasn't felt in years, since she was a kid and everyone used to go barefoot all over the place. Why don't people do that anymore? She tests her toes on the pavement, liking the directness of the energy, the benevolence of the earth beneath the thin layer of asphalt, beneath her soles. She looks up; the morning haze has burnt off, and the sun is high in a relatively blue sky. Mabel goes off to Broadway to find Mason and Beth. Perhaps she'll pick up a dozen bagels for lunch, too and they'll have a picnic in celebration.

Sam drives the rectangle of treed streets reading the signs from Fir to Pine to Burrard (is Burrard a type of tree? He doesn't know). Cypress to Maple to Arbutus (his favourite kind of tree, with its twisting smooth trunks and red bark) to Yew to Vine to Balsam to Larch (nice, also; unusual) to Trafalgar. Trafalgar? *That* he knows is no tree. Burrard probably isn't either. And he's been up and down MacDonald Street, which is the next one over, a thousand times. How far could Beth have gotten? Perhaps she's got a concussion and has wandered into some stranger's house unknowingly looking for help or the boy. There's something about the boy in the hoodie on Broadway that bothers him. Not that the boy looked even close to being nine years old, but a boy and his father on the street selling newspapers? Surely someone would call Social Services, wouldn't they? You wouldn't just let that one go, would you? Would he? He looks across at Laurel, who is filing a broken nail.

"What did you think about that boy?" Sam asks.

"Which one? The blonde or the one with the maple leaf shaved into the back of his head?" Laurel stops filing and looks over at Sam. She wouldn't have thought Sam would have noticed whom she was sitting with at the other table, unless he was interested after all? Then she remembers her dishrag hand. He's probably gay, she thinks, the good ones usually are.

"The boy at the newsstand next to Benny's," Sam says.

"Christ, I could use a beer and a bagel, I'm famished," Laurel says.

Sam looks at her. Her mascara is smudged; her hair is a blonde puff of disarray. She has dim circles under her eyes. She could be Bella Lugosi's girlfriend. She does look famished. Perhaps it's time to throw in the towel and the Fluevogs and get Laurel, who has sobered up after vomiting in the bushes several times and sleeping through most of his search-and-rescue effort, to simply drop him off at his home in Point Grey. He thinks now she could legally blow a breathalyser and drive dangerously well. Laurel can give Beth her shoes back on Tuesday at Dairyland, and they can both call it a night. He's tired and the cocaine has made him ravenous. But the thought of his wrist and Beth's mind makes him do another loop around Broadway. He wants one more look at that boy.

Beth comes to, a swimmer breaking the surface of a still-cold lake on a May long weekend. A twenty-year-old swimmer who's got a whole life ahead of her. The prospect of a wonderful husband, a couple of kids, a nice house somewhere that, even though it's got a missing baseboard in the kitchen and a chunk of cement about to fall off the outside wall by the front door, she'll love anyway, because it's home. Her home – full of love and more laughter than is really fair in one person's life and someone else breathing beside her at night. She rubs her face and feels a large scab on her left cheek. Right. It's the Queen's birthday, she remembers, as if royalty were important in the here and now next to the rank rising smell of the produce decomposing in the blue bin beside her. She sits up and looks around. The shops are all open now. People are moving along the sidewalks. Life is in full swing. She's slept an hour, possibly more? She must have been exhausted. The sun is hot on her head. The thickening smell makes her nauseous. She pushes her mangled aluminum chair off her and remembers Mason. The boy she's been missing all her life.

She stands up too swiftly and stars come to her head like she's been hit with a baseball bat. She wobbles and has to hang onto the bin for support. Two teenage girls walk past and give her a *look*. Get lost, Beth wants to holler at them. You don't know anything. You're young; you haven't worked at Dairyland or anywhere yet for seventeen years straight. You don't even know what a mortgage payment is other than something your parents fret about when they lie in bed late at night when by rights they should be making love and not averting financial disasters. You have no clue what it's like to sleep with fifty-four men and women out there in the dating field (really, could it be fifty-four? When the national average is less than a third of her age?) and find not one good enough to take home and keep. All she really wants is one mate. A husband, she decides, because Maple is truly spoken for. One husband, forty-seven different ways and as many times as it takes to make a blissful life. You have no idea; she wants to tell the two girls. Not a blessed inkling, so go plant your teenaged butt on a bar stool and hope to hell you get someone before it's too late.

Her head is reeling with the heat. She takes a deep breath. She may be dehydrated. Maybe that's the reason she feels so irrational. That and the fact that life can change in a helluva hurry. One day she's hauling in the overtime, reasonably happy these last few months since she swore off dating and is no longer subjecting herself to rejection and the act of rejecting, both equally humiliating. Or planning her next pair of Fluevogs, a great tan and black Brothel-creeper that she saw a week ago in the store on Granville. Or that if things go right and overtime is as consistent at Dairyland as it has been, she could conceivably pay her house off in four more years. And now today she's out grappling with a blue bin and her best friend's nine-year-old boy is missing. And all of it is her fault. How could this have happened? She lets go of the bin and sees a pair of abandoned pink sandals. How convenient. She rips off her filthy sweat socks and pitches them into the bin and slides her sore feet into the sun-warmed sandals. Then she steps forward and trips on a can of guava juice. She kicks it across the alley, and the two teenaged girls turn and look at her as if she's truly a hazard to society. This time she can't rein herself in and gives them the finger.

Mabel turns the corner onto Broadway and finds Mason holding up a copy of *Word on the Street*, which she normally buys whenever she comes down from Kerrisdale to buy bagels.

"Mason!" Mabel says in pure delight. She kneels down on the sidewalk and wraps her mother body around him. She feels his thinness in her arms, like hugging a crow, nothing but a mesh of down and feathers with not much weight beneath. She's never noticed how undersized Mason is, how skeletal he feels. But then, he's spent a night on the street. She supposes he might feel this way out of sheer authenticity. Mabel straightens up and holds Mason by his shoulders so she can look at him. Check out the effects of a homeless night. He looks into Mabel's eyes and doesn't say a word.

His dark eyes look tired, but not overly so. Mabel clutches his face in her smooth hands and kisses his forehead until he pulls away from her. Mason looks up at Kenneth. Mabel glances at Kenneth and smiles politely, and then looks around for Beth. She doesn't see her anywhere. Possibly she's gone into Benny's next door to use the washroom or into the Chinese for a bottle of cranberry juice?

"Mason, where is Beth?" his mother asks. Mason is

silent. Surely Beth's disappearance has something to do with him, doesn't it? Something he's done? He's caused a small but noticeable tear in the universe and now Beth has gone missing. Largely due to what? The White Spot? Hostess Ding Dongs? Coca-a-cola? He can't figure out the cause but the effect is – is that Beth is missing. It may make his mother frantic. Mason stares back at his mother in silence. Mabel looks up at Kenneth, clearly this time; no polite smile.

"Is he with you?" she asks Mason, but doesn't take her eyes off Kenneth. Kenneth avoids her gaze and tilts a copy of the newspaper towards her. But no, she is not deterred. She shifts her interrogation light back onto Mason.

"What are you doing out here? Where is Beth? Is this part of it? This selling of newspapers?" Mabel pulls Mason close to her now, so that even if he would answer, he can't because his face is buried somewhere about Mabel's waist. Mabel glances at Kenneth again.

"Is that the man from your school?" she asks.

Mason nods in the folds of her plaid spring skirt.

"Well!" Mabel says, and then says it again without the exclamation mark. "Well, hello," Mabel nods.

Kenneth dips his head toward her.

"So you are Kenneth?" Mabel asks, seeing his embroidered coat.

"My name is William," Kenneth says. "I live in Kerrisdale."

"Yes, I do, too," Mabel smiles. "You live behind Oakdale Elementary?"

"That's where I live," William says, with nary a mention of Kenmore Styrofoam boxes or brown bag lunches.

"Well, thank you, William, for waiting with my son while Beth . . ." Mabel's voice fades off.

William shrugs, no big deal, he's here for the duration. Besides, the boy found him. Not the other way around. Seems he got up to go for a piss and got lost. When he came back the woman he was with was gone.

Mabel surveys the street for Beth. Certainly Beth can't be far away. Mason stands upright now and takes his mother's hand.

"I'm hungry," Mason says, without the benefit of his mother's ear. "I'd like some breakfast."

Mabel looks down at him, his face is earnest and sure, exactly the boy she's been waiting all these years for him to grow into. He tugs on her hand and they go into Benny's.

It's noon, and the lunch trade, which should be bustling, isn't. William notices that Mason chooses a table near the front so he can watch him sell newspapers. He probably wants to see how many people notice William's photo on the front page. It's become a kind of joke between the two of them. A way for William to quell Mason's fear that he can sense mounting as the minutes tick dutifully along with the arcing sun and still no sign of the woman he came with. Like going to Wal-Mart and losing sight of the person who brought you, and then you end up standing at the front door like an orphan or a missing child, with both the Wal-Mart Greeter who's seventy-four, and the underpaid security guard who's thirty-four, looking for whomever you came with. So William makes a show of holding the newspaper up like a magician practised in the art of distraction, then someone comes along and buys a copy, glances at both the photo and William, and here's where William looks down and winks at Mason beneath his hoodie as if to say, *let's see*. Then the person walks off down the street. Not a word of recognition, not a backward glance, not even paying attention. Mason grins back. So far only one person has noticed, the man in the Italian leather shoes who paid him a toonie.

Sam looks up as Mabel stands in line at the counter waiting to order. Lovely, Sam thinks. Great skin, nice-looking, too. Like Beth. Sam sees the boy in the hoodie go and sit at the counter by the front window. Did they come in together? Wasn't that the same boy he'd come back to check on and was nowhere to be found? Though this boy looks taller, more like a nine-year-old. Sam nudges Laurel with his elbow to look at the boy. Laurel doesn't care; she's hungry and tired. She orders two bagels with raspberry jam and a Sleeman's. She doesn't ask Sam what he wants. Then she gets up and goes to the restroom.

Mabel looks towards the back of the restaurant, a quick search for the whereabouts of Beth. Where *is* she? And how did Mason come to be out front selling newspapers with the homeless man from his school?

Did they plan this? Was this part of the homeless experience and *where is Beth*? Did she duck home for a quick shower and was going to be right back? How could Beth leave Mason in the care of a homeless man, familiar or not? Mabel thinks about that and finds she can't muster the full fury that should naturally follow. She's worn down from a sleepless night and in general from beating the jumbled, malevolent world off her doorstep each day. She finds that she's ready to blow her thin Rubbermaid lid of broadmindedness up to the top of Benny's ceiling.

It's her turn to order. She steps forward but not before the young man behind the counter, who not only looks like but *could be* Kurt Cobain's ghost come to serve her kosher bagels, notices her attractive but bare feet.

"Sorry ma'am," he says, "I can't serve you."

He points at the sign on the door. No Shirt, No Shoes, No Service. He looks at her, appreciating that she's got a scoop neck t-shirt on and is a hot-looking woman even without shoes, but rules are rules. His boss is standing in the back rolling out dough. And if he didn't look like Kurt Cobain, he might have let her off, let her buy a dozen bagels and a pot of Winnipeg Cream Cheese blessed on the end of an assembly line by a bona fide rabbi, but he's new here and on probation and his thin greasy blonde hair doesn't endear him to his boss, who while rolling out dough is also paying attention with his peripheral vision. Besides: you let one, then you've got a whole truckload of shoeless players coming in and wanting to be served bagels. Had she come in shirtless, Kurt might have had to rethink whether or not his probation was worth it.

"I know," Mabel says. This kid is half her age and she certainly doesn't need him to point out what she already knows about food and public sanitation. But this is an exception, she's not some homeless character straight off the street, she's a stem cell research scientist and she knows full well the repercussions of letting just anyone in without proper footgear.

"I left them in the alley for someone who is sleeping there."

"That's great, but I can't serve you."

"I've come in to buy some bagels with my son. Look," Mabel points to the front window where Mason is sitting. "He's got his *goddamn* shoes on."

"No need to swear, ma'am," Kurt says beneath his stringy hair, though it's apparent from the slight smirk on his face that he's heard a lot worse. "It's not my fault, ma'am."

If he calls her ma'am once more, she's going to come across the counter and stuff a multigrain bagel down his skinny neck. And where the hell is Beth? Mabel looks towards the restroom door. A woman comes out and sits down beside a silver-haired man who seems keenly interested in what's going on at the front where Mason is.

Mabel wants to ask the silver-haired man what his problem is, but her Rubbermaid lid has already slipped out *goddamn* and she finds herself without voice.

Beth walks in the open door. She looks like she's been out on a bender. Her brown bobbed hair is appalling; she's got something green stuck in her hair along with her blonde streaks. Is that romaine lettuce? Blonde streaks! The woman she gave her sandals to? And can of guava juice? The sleeping woman beside the dumpster out back whom she entrusted her son with? She's got dried blood all over her left cheek and — Mabel looks down at Beth's feet — *she's* got shoes on,

Mabel's pink, sturdy, clear plastic sandals recycled wholly from pop bottles. She's also got a bent aluminum chair tucked under her arm.

"Can I help you, ma'am?" Kurt Cobain says, looking straight past Mabel like she's been dealt out of the game and now he's moving on.

"Beth!"

A chorus of *Beth!*s from the restaurant: the table at the back, Mabel at the counter, and a normally silent Mason.

Mason, oh my god, Mason. Beth rushes over to the front counter and hugs Mason with every inch of her thirty-six years, every fibre of humility that she has left. Thank god, he's alive. She realizes this is the hug she should have given both herself and him last night when their stuff got jacked. All anyone wants is someone to hang onto, she thinks. Mason doesn't flinch back or pull away, either. When Beth releases him, Mason is smiling his bunny teeth full-throttle at her. She hugs him again and laughs until she cries.

Beth glances towards the back of Benny's past Maple in the line-up. She can't bear the look of fear and bewilderment on Maple's face. Through her tears, Beth can make out the sun-glowing silhouetted forms of her friend Laurel and the great guy she met last night. *Beth* met last night. Well, Bravo! for Laurel, Beth thinks, with a twinge of envy. He was hers. Or he could have been hers, had she not been such a mess. Had she met him one week earlier.

And if Beth were not standing in front of Maple, whose aura has all the qualities of a mother bear separated from her beloved cub, Beth might have wished exactly that. That time itself turn back one week, a few days even, and Beth might have a second chance not to do anything rash, like take a nine-year-old boy out to sleep on the streets of Vancouver. Or lose her head and her shoes and her fleece. She notices now that Mason has her fleece on and someone has rolled the sleeves up to make it manageable. In the same instant that Beth hopes for time to turn itself back, she also hopes it will speed on ahead past this horrible moment, this terrible collision of universes devoid of homogeny.

Beth spots her Fluevogs under the table by Sam's feet. She touches her left breast and feels the paper package on the inside pocket of the coat and her right lung aches faintly, but then her fingertips find the embroidered letters S A M, and her heart sinks a little deeper in her chest cavity.

To make matters worse, the manager comes over and informs Maple that, while he's sorry and she's good-looking (he actually says this), he's going to have to ask her to leave. He points to the sign on the door. No Shirt, No Shoes, No Service. No Staying, while unwritten, is apparently implicit.

Mabel looks at Beth. Whereas Mason has spoken twice now without the aid of her ear, she is rendered wordless for the second time. She stares at Beth like she can hardly believe what is going on. Here's Beth with lettuce (Mabel is sure now – *it is romaine*) in her hair and a mangled chair beneath her arm (is that Mabel's chair?) looking to the entire seeing world like a vagrant straight from the company of a blue bin, wearing Mabel's pink plastic sandals, and Kurt at the counter is ready to serve *her*? Simply because *she* has shoes on? Can he not see Beth? She has produce in her hair. And this is the woman she has entrusted with her Mason?

Mason slides down from his stool and takes Beth's hand. He leads her over beside his mother and slips his other hand into his mother's. Mabel looks surprised.

She wonders whose coat Mason has on. Mason peers up at Beth from beneath his hoodie and her fleece and smiles again. The benevolence of his smile floods over Beth and her sleepless night wandering the streets in search of not only Mason but also every other man/woman she's ever lost, too. Grief lives in the house of accumulation like a whole lot of unused wool gathered and stored — why, she could probably knit an entire leisure suit. God knows what Mason has had to endure in her absence. Beth stands, battered-down but responsible, in front of stunning, shoeless Maple. Tears fill her eyes again and run down her cheeks, mixing with the dried blood.

Sam gets up from his table. Laurel is eating her double order of bagels and taking slugs on her Sleeman's while she watches the goings-on like she's at the matinee. Sam picks up the shoes beneath the table and walks across the restaurant.

"Will these be all right?" Sam says to the manager, who looks dismayed, as if Sam has produced a black tie and dinner jacket just right for the occasion.

Laurel lets out a loud guffaw from the back of Benny's. Everyone turns and looks at her. She raises up her bottle of Sleeman's and toasts them.

Beth stares at Sam. Sam smiles and smoothes his hand across the small of her back. Beth sees that she may be wrong. It's not Bravo! for Laurel but perhaps Bravo! for her? Was all this intentional, Beth wonders? A coming together of time and happenstance in order to show her something? Purposeful, Beth can handle, but chaos makes her want to throw herself into another seventeen years straight of overtime at Dairyland and pay her house off and live lonely ever after with married renters above her head making love every third night and twice on the weekends. Much less complicated that way. Still, Mason is here and he doesn't look too terrible. Maple is here as well. Timing on your side and happychance thrown in for good measure? How did that happen? Beth looks closely at Mason and thinks she detects the remnants of chocolate sponge cake on Mason's mouth. So many questions, such a private boy, Beth thinks. She finds herself gripping his scrawny hand all the more.

Mabel looks at the silver-haired man with the shoes. The same man that was intensely interested in her son up until a moment ago. Now he is offering her a pair of shoes. Good, solid shoes, from the looks of them, green-swirled suede, thick soles. Mabel looks from Beth to Mason. Both of them nod their heads in approval. The silver-haired man sets the shoes down at Mabel's feet and she slides one foot in, then the other.

"Wrong princess," Laurel yells out from the back of Benny's and laughs unaccompanied. Mabel, who doesn't know Laurel, ignores her. Beth, who knows Laurel all too well, knows enough to ignore her in the hope that Laurel isn't tempted to launch into the particulars of last night, of which even Beth isn't sure of all the sordid details. Like: how did Mason end up in Benny's? And Maple? And Sam, who Beth thought must have come back for Laurel when Beth turned out to be a Danger!, a Detour, a No Exit. Sam's hand on the small of her back makes her think otherwise.

Mason's hand firmly in hers makes Beth believe that when the truth does come out, eventually over time all this will be another life/adventure story where everyone got out alive and in one piece on the other end, much like being chained to a hundred-year-old tree up in Clayoquot Sound and making the front page of the *Vancouver Sun*. Or perhaps written about by a beardless writer on MacDonald Street. Then even Maple will forgive her. Mason looks up at Beth and she chucks him under the chin.

The manager shakes his head and goes behind the counter to roll out bagel dough.

Kurt steps forward and addresses Mabel in her Fluevogs as if she's a brand new customer.

"Can I help you, ma'am?"

Mabel orders a dozen multigrain bagels and asks Mason if he's ever had a chocolate chip bagel and if, as a special treat, would he like one today? It's the Queen's birthday, she says. Satan's brother-in-law is away for the long weekend.

"Yes," Mason says out loud and by himself.

"Yes!" Mabel says like it's a celebration. What the hell – she orders half a dozen.

Out in front of Benny's, the sun is shining full circle now. William is in front of the Chinese grocer, and whether anyone notices he is the Seller of the Year doesn't matter. He's holding his head a little higher. It's the coat. The coat has made him visible. He's on the map, he's a mini-blip on the human radar screen and the next time someone calls him Kenneth, he will correct them and tell them the name his mother gave him, William. German, like his absent father. William, meaning resolute guardian.

Mason goes to the open door and watches William hold up the *Word on The Street*.

Mason watches people buy the thin newspaper and walk away, oblivious.

"You like children?" Sam asks Beth.

"O, yes," Beth says, "very much."

Acknowledgements

I want to thank: The Senior Belts for their expert flaying and on-going support: Marina Endicott, Steve Gobby, Jeanne Harvie and Susan Kelly. Saint Pete from Seventeenth, who has been both on the street and in my psyche for more years than I can count. My phone-a-friend and locations advisor, Keath Fraser. The Banff Center for the Arts: Carol Holmes and of course, Fred Stenson. Curtis Gillespie for his fine tutelage and keen eyes, both of them. The Alberta Arts Foundation for their financial support. My many able-minded readers: Dani Kvern for endings, Bobbie Charron for enthusiastic support, Kelly and Erin Gray for their readership. Nola Fielding, fellow creator, my mother, Barbara Kvern, for being my mother, my mother-in-law, Beverly Rasporich, for the same reason, my grandmother-in-law, Irene Matson, who overlooked both drug usage and profane language. My like-named editor, Lee Shedden, whose electric guidance and well-honed sense of humour gave me much currency. My husband, Paul Rasporich, for the Degas book cover. Ken Richardson for taking excellent photographs year after year. Anyone out there who spends a portion of his or her day creating something (thanks to Steven Soderbergh for that); while it may not do much for the coffers, it provides much fodder for the soul. And lastly, my Kai and Seth and Paul Rasporich, who are fodder for my soul.